FLASH

THE LION

A

The guide stopped still. 'We must hurry,' he said after a few seconds of nervous listening.

'What is it? inquired Flash.

Harn trotted down the trail. 'The night brings many dangers,' he said.

From off to the right came a loud thrashing.

Then Flash saw one of the creatures. It looked like a salamander – but it was nine feet long, and opened its huge mouth to reveal gleaming snake-like fangs.

With a few more lumbering steps of its four squatty feet, the giant salamander blocked their path completely. Its mouth gaped open, showing the curved fangs and a huge split tongue.

'It will devour us!' cried Harn.

Also in this exciting series to be published in *Star*

FLASH GORDON 2 : THE PLAGUE OF SOUND
FLASH GORDON 3 : THE SPACE CIRCUS
FLASH GORDON 4 : THE TIME TRAP OF MING XIII
FLASH GORDON 5 : THE WITCH QUEEN OF MONGO
FLASH GORDON 6 : THE WAR OF THE CYBERNAUTS

FLASH GORDON I
THE LION MEN OF MONGO

Alex Raymond's Original Story

Adapted by Con Steffanson

A STAR BOOK

published by

the Paperback Division of

W. H. ALLEN & Co. Ltd

A Star Book
Published in 1977
by the Paperback Division of W. H. Allen & Co. Ltd
A Howard and Wyndham Company
123 King Street, London W6 9JG

Printed in Great Britain by
Hazell Watson & Viney Ltd, Aylesbury, Bucks

ISBN 0 352 39570 2

The Lion Men of Mongo

CHAPTER ONE

Everything went well until ten minutes before set-down time.

The interplanet survey ship then began to have trouble. The temperature in the oval control chamber started to climb rapidly, at first half a degree at a time, then in jumps of five and ten degrees. The central control panel grew stove-hot, tiny wisps of acrid blue smoke uncoiled from some of the grids and rows of bubble lights.

Dr. Zarkov, a big burly man with a furious black beard, had been bent over the scanning monitors studying the multiple views of the terrain of the planet they were about to land on. "Palmaceae," he had said in his booming voice. "Excessively large, but palm trees nonetheless, exactly as I expected. And there are stands of large cypress-like trees. Yes, what I anticipated. What's this now?" He squinted, putting his broad face nearer to the center viewing screen in the bank of five. "Yes, *chrysopsis mariana* and *hieracium scabum*. But unlike those of our own Earth System of planets, where they grow to heights of eight or ten feet, these devils are twenty feet tall if they're an inch." He gave a chesty chuckle, rubbing his knobby hands together.

"Did you also," asked Dale Arden, "expect trouble with our ship?" She was a slim girl in her middle twenties, dark-haired, wearing a lightweight, pale blue jumpsuit.

Zarkov blinked, looking up at his research assistant. "What's that?"

Dale, seated on the edge of her inflated plyochair, pointed in the direction of the control panels. "How serious is it, Flash?"

In the piloting seat, Flash Gordon shook his head, keeping his eyes on the controls in front of him. "Don't know," he said. "I'm switching over to the backup systems and we'll see." He was a tall, broad-shouldered man, a year away from thirty, with blond hair and an even, outdoor tan.

Zarkov bounded across the cabin, his work boots thumping on the noryl-plastic flooring. "There can't be anything wrong," he boomed. "I designed this ship myself, equipped it especially for this pioneer exploration of Mongo."

The heat in the metal-walled room kept jumping higher. More smoke was pluming up out of the control panels.

"I can't get any response from the landing mechanisms, can't punch up a landing pattern, though I don't see why." Flash made one further jab at a series of toggle switches to his left. "All frozen, including the backups."

"Impossible," said Zarkov as he dropped to his knees. "But since the impossible seems to be happening, we'll have to use our second set of backups." He pushed down a row of switches below the ones Flash was struggling with. "There."

"Still nothing," Flash told him after a second. "We don't seem to have any control over the ship."

Stretching up and whipping an electric screwdriver out of a hip pocket in his one-piece worksuit, Zarkov attacked a panel in the cabin's low ceiling. "I made test flights in this damn ship myself, back on our base planet. I can't . . ." He got the plate unscrewed, tossed it aside and thrust one big rough hand into the opening. "This is something akin to open-heart massage. It should, I believe, get our landing mechanisms going again."

Flash waited five seconds more, then said, "Everything's still frozen, Doc."

Dale had risen and was standing beside Flash. She touched his shoulder with one slender hand. "Looks like we'll have to ditch."

"Ridiculous," snorted Zarkov, holstering his screwdriver. "I designed this craft to be foolproof, which I guarantee it is." He gave his ample beard a tug. "Besides which, I sank nearly all of the PlanExplo Foundation's last grant into building this crate. If it smashes up, there's twenty million bucks in a pile of rubble."

"Dale's right, Doc," said Flash. "It's either ditch or crash."

"I can't let—"

"Okay, look," cut in the tall blond man, "you and Dale get out. I'll keep fiddling. That way you two are safe and maybe we can save the ship, too."

The girl's hand tightened on his shoulder. "There's no point, Flash, it's too dangerous," she said. "Even if we lose the ship, all we have to do to get off the planet is radio back to Dr. Zarkov's orbiting workshop and one of his robots will—"

"If it looks like I can't save the ship, I'll radio and get them to send a rescue craft," Flash assured her. "But I want to try to save this thing first. Now you and Doc get ready to use the escape tube."

"This isn't right, Flash," protested Zarkov in his booming voice. "As the designer of the ship, I should stick with her."

Flash grinned. "It's the captain who's supposed to go down with his ship."

Dale had sprinted to a wall cabinet and was breaking out three flying safety belts. "There's one here for you, Flash."

Reluctantly Zarkov strapped on the device. "These belts are based on my own designs, remember? So they'll register the exact place where Dale and I land on your rescue monitor there."

Nodding, Flash said, "Once I get the ship safely down, I'll come back for you."

"Good, good," boomed the bearded scientist. "We'll stay exactly where we land and wait for you."

After strapping on the flying belt, Dale bent and kissed Flash gently on the cheek. "We'll see you soon."

"I guarantee it," he said, using one of the doctor's favorite phrases.

The slim girl crossed to the trap door of the escape tube. She dropped from sight and was ejected from the craft.

"Twenty million isn't everything," reminded Zarkov as he approached the tube hatch. "So don't be too foolhardy, Flash. If you figure you can't bring her down, jump too."

"Don't worry, Doc."

The heat inside the survey ship's cabin was now up to a hundred and twenty degrees, according to the temperature gauge on the control panel. Smoke was swirling thickly.

Flash continued to struggle with the buttons, switches and toggles of the intricate control board. There was still no response.

Five minutes after Dale and Zarkov had jumped free, Flash finally pushed up out of the piloting seat. "Doc and PlanExplo won't like this, but I'm going to have to give up and get out." He noted the positions where Dale and the doctor had landed. Then he strapped on his flying belt and started toward the radio-communications panel in the far wall to get in touch with the robots on their orbiting workshop.

But before he reached it, the ship began to wobble wildly, flames howled out of the control board, and then the ship was plummeting down toward the ground.

CHAPTER TWO

They were coming in through the gaps and rents in the twisted metal, in through the sprung emergency door.

Slithering down the pocked walls, crawling over the black smeared control panels toward the blond man stretched out on the cabin floor. Snake-like, but a watery orange in color with red-rimmed suction pads running up and down their doughy bellies. Two dozen of them, each six feet long, oozing across the floor of the crashed survey ship, forked tongues flicking out through jagged fangs.

Flash groaned, stirring, his left hand flexing and unflexing. He lay sprawled on his back.

The lead reptile was now within a yard of him. It began to form an angle, its head rising up and swaying.

Opening his eyes and seeing this nightmare, Flash murmured, "I wonder if Zarkov was expecting anything like this." Very carefully he worked his right hand down to his holster. He eased out his blaster pistol and pointed it at the swaying creature. "Back," he warned.

The reptile's head jerked as it prepared to strike.

Flash fired the pistol.

There was a sizzling crackling sound and the head that had been jabbing through the air was gone. For an instant, a sooty image hung there, then it vanished to nothing.

A second dull orange reptile poised to attack Flash. Again the blaster pistol crackled.

The other creatures halted. In another moment, they were quivering away, squeezing out of the ruined ship through the holes and tears in its metal sides. Each of them left a wide trail of pale blue slime behind.

Dodging the crisscross of slimey trails, Flash went to the radio-communications wall. "Not exactly a perfect setdown," he said as he surveyed the wrecked cabin.

He found that the communications equipment, too, was ruined, meaning there was no way to report the crash. The robots in the orbiting lab were not programmed to initiate a rescue on their own. An economy measure Dr. Zarkov had reluctantly decided on.

Flash swiftly made a circuit of the cabin, determining what equipment could be salvaged. There was nothing, unfortunately, to enable him to communicate with the flying workshop. He decided he would leave most of the portable equipment and food supplies here for the moment. In a plyo rucksack, he packed emergency rations, two extra blaster pistols and a few other gadgets. They could come back for the rest later. He attached a hunting knife to his belt.

It was midafternoon outside. Flash guessed he'd been unconscious for an hour. "Dale and Doc should still be waiting for me, though."

Walking to the emergency door, which hung lopsidedly open, he looked out. He saw a stretch of tough brownish grass, the boles of huge palm trees. Dozens of gold insects were swirling low to the ground. There was no sign of the reptiles who had made a try for him.

Flash took a deep breath before dropping out of the ship and down to the soil of Mongo.

The air was humid, fuzzy.

He stood on the rough grass, looking up at the bright alien sun. Then he checked his compass, nodded to himself, and set off to find Zarkov and Dale.

A new spacewarp process, perfected in part by Dr. Zarkov himself, had recently opened up the Mongo System of planets to exploration. Prior to that, they had been too distant from Earth and the other planets who shared her sun.

With Dale and Flash, Zarkov had already explored one of Mongo's sister planets. He had determined that all the planets in this system were life-supporting and that all of them might have humanoid inhabitants and fairly advanced cultures.

"He didn't say anything about those snakes, though," Flash said to himself as he worked his way through the twisting, twining underbrush which cluttered the spaces between the enormous palm trees.

High above him, a hundred feet or more, giant palm fronds met to make a bright green roof over much of the jungle below. A profusion of giant butterflies, hundreds of them, wheeled and glided high up. They were scarlet, silver, bright blue, and glaring white, passing through dark shadows and stripes of intense hazy sunlight. Near and far, birds called in falsetto hoots and tinny squawks.

After nearly fifteen minutes, Flash noticed he was approaching some kind of trail. "Manmade, too," he guessed.

The road cut through the thick jungle. It was roughly thirty feet wide, dusty.

He calculated this road should lead him fairly close to the spot where Dr. Zarkov should have come down. "Provided his flying belt is working a little better than his survey ship."

A sad-eyed monkey calmly watched him pass. It hung by its tail from a low branch of a gnarled tree beside the roadway. It was the size of a three-year-old child, covered with fine silvery hair.

When Flash had been traveling for over an hour, he paused. "I covered quite a bit of ground before the ship cracked up," he said to himself. "Looks like I'm not going to hit the first rendezvous spot for a while yet."

From up ahead, he heard something. The road curved and he couldn't see around the bend. There came a dry creaking sound and a forlorn rattling.

Flash moved into the brush again, working his way cautiously around the bend.

On the far side of the road, he saw a huge twisted oak-like tree.

A dead man was hanging from the tree.

CHAPTER THREE

The dead man had been hanging there a good while. Birds and insects and time had been at work on him. The thick chains which held his wrists and ankles together were rusted, the rope which had broken his neck was now a greasy black. His clothes had lost most of their resemblance to clothes and were filthy strips and tatters.

But the sign in crude black letters tacked to his chest was still quite legible: *He possessed a forbidden weapon.*

Flash stood looking up at the gently swaying corpse. "So there are men on this planet," he reflected. "They don't treat each other very well, and to have a weapon is a hanging crime."

He resumed his trek. He tapped the holster at his side. "I wonder what kind of weapons are forbidden." He unfastened the holster, removed the blaster, and thrust the holster back into his rucksack. The gun he stuck in his waistband where his tunic hid it from sight.

Five miles further along the road, he saw another dead man hanging from a tree. This man had not been dead as long as the other one. He had been hanged and chained in the same way.

The sign on his chest announced: *Executed by order of Emperor Ming. He stole food.*

"A very harsh society we've dropped into," Flash said to himself. "To kill a man for taking food." He walked on, looking back once over his shoulder. "Be interesting to see what kind of reception this Emperor Ming gives us if we ever meet him."

After a few more minutes, he added, "At any rate, Zarkov will be happy to know his lingual-translator works." Prior to the initial trip to the Mongo System of planets, the doctor had had a microminiaturized device implanted in Flash, Dale, and himself. He guaranteed it would translate any written or spoken language they encountered and enable them to respond in kind.

Eventually, the light of the late afternoon began to fade. A fuzzy darkness slowly filled the jungle.

Flash halted. "This should be just about the spot Zarkov came down," he said as he glanced around. "Dale will be further on."

The flying belt was designed so that the wearer could control his descent. Unless something had gone wrong, the doctor would have been able to set himself down on a clear spot on the road and not in among the tangle of trees and brush.

But he was not here.

"Zarkov," Flash called through cupped hands. "Doc, are you around? Hey, Zarkov."

Three crimson birds rattled up out of the brush, flew off into the gathering dark.

"Zarkov. Doc."

Flash noticed something stuck on a thorny bush at the roadside. It was a shred of cloth. He plucked it free, a tough tan material. "Torn from Zarkov's worksuit," he said. "And this looks like a splash of blood on it."

From his rucksack, he took a small round flashlight which fit into the palm of his hand. Near the place he'd found the bloodstained swatch he discovered footprints. "Yes, Doc's boot made that one for sure. These other ones, though, they're sandals of some kind." A few yards further along were signs of a struggle, footprints intersecting, brush trampled, branches broken. "But no more blood, which is maybe a good sign."

Flash bent to study the footprints. "Two or three big men at least. Well, it would take that many to overpower Zarkov." He swept the beam of his palmlight over the road. "Now let's see where they took him."

There were indications the men who'd attacked Dr. Zarkov had carried him across the road. Brush and tall ferns had been pushed aside to allow passage into the jungle.

Shining the light into the thickness of the darkening forest, Flash decided, "That's going to be a tough trail to follow. I'd better find Dale first. This jungle doesn't seem too hospitable a place even in broad daylight. No telling what it'll be like after dark."

He clicked off the light and started to run, at a steady jog, along the road.

The night closed in, killing the last of the twilight.

There was a clearing to the right of the road at the location where Dale should have landed. An oval pool lay in the center of the clearing. Frogs croaked hollowly beyond the pool's far edge.

"Dale, it's Flash. Are you here?"

A rustling commenced along the trees next to the pool.

"Dale, is that you?"

Out of the dark, a raspy voice said, "If you seek the young woman, I can tell you where they took her."

CHAPTER FOUR

It was a small bent man who spoke to Flash across the jungle pool. He wore a simple mud-colored tunic laced with leather strings, rough-spun tights and low boots of soft hide. His hair was long and unkempt, speckled with gray. Several of his lower front teeth were missing. "You are an outlander," he observed in his harsh raspy voice, "as was the girl."

Flash, keeping his light shining on the man, circled the pool. There didn't seem to be anyone else lurking in the woods. "You saw the girl?"

"Oh, yes," replied the bent man. "Saw her as clear as I'm seeing you now. Nay, clearer since it was still day. A pretty girl, with dark hair. Too pretty, that's the trouble."

"What do you mean?"

"I mean, outlander, that is why they took her."

Stopping a few feet from the man Flash asked, "Who was it that took her?"

"The Royal Police it was." He rubbed at his sharp chin. "Tied her up and carried her off on his saddle, did the captain of police."

"She was arrested?"

The bent man gave a dry wheezing laugh. "Too pretty for that, didn't I tell you. No, outlander, they took her to the capital. You see, our emperor is always interested in pretty young girls and many's the maiden who's been dragged away to the Imperial Palace."

"You're talking about the Emperor Ming?"

"Aye, Ming, ruler of the Dozen Territories," he said. "And soon, if he carries out all his plans, ruler of all the planet."

"How long ago did they take her?"

"There is no chance to catch them," said the bent man, "should that be what you're thinking of. True they were on horseback, the two Royal Police who took her. By now, though, they have placed her aboard a flying ship and flown her to Ming's palace."

"How far from here is the capital city?"

"Three hundred miles."

"Where can I arrange to fly there?"

The bent man's rasping laugh was louder this time. "Would you end your life hanging from one of these trees, outlander?" he replied.

"You mean the use of airships is forbidden, too?"

"To all save the Royal Police and those in the emperor's inner circle," the bent man explained. "If you would journey to the capital, however, I can show you the best route to take. My name is Harn, and I ofttimes serve as a guide."

Flash decided that he wouldn't go back and follow the trail of Dr. Zarkov, not now at any rate. The burly scientist was capable of taking care of himself for a while. It was Dale he must find, as soon as possible. "Very well," he told Harn, "I'll accept your offer."

"My usual fee, outlander, is five mingots a day."

"I have none of your local money."

Eyeing the pack strapped to the tall man's back, Harn said, "Perhaps you have some goods, some objects of value from your own land which can be exchanged for coins. There is an inn not far from here, the Heart & Arrow, and the innkeeper is a longtime friend of mine. He, even in these lean times, usually has a supply of ready cash to pay out for certain marketable items."

After studying the man's lean wrinkled face for a few seconds, Flash said, "All right, the Heart & Arrow it is."

A thick mist was spreading through the trees, streaking the dark with gray. The night sounds were muffled, dimmed. "Is there water close by?" Flash asked his guide.

"Aye," replied Harn, "we are but a mile or so from the Great River." He was walking a few feet ahead of Flash.

"Can I follow the river to the capital?"

"Perhaps. Do not fear, outlander, I will see you reach the destination you seek," promised the bent man. "The Heart & Arrow Inn sits beside the river and when we reach it, I will help you chart your course."

The river fog was chill. It was rolling in more rapidly now, filling the spaces between the giant tree trunks, covering the mossy ground.

"You were indeed lucky," said Harn after a moment, "that I encountered you this night. Very few dare venture through this jungle once darkness has fallen."

"Why is that—is it haunted?"

"Jest if you will, outlander, but—" The guide stopped still. "We must hurry," he said after a few seconds of nervous listening.

"What is it?"

Harn began trotting along the narrow trail they'd been following. "The night brings many dangers with it," he said over his shoulder.

From off to their right came a loud thrashing.

"Which particular danger are we running from?"

"It sounded to my ears very much like a salamander."

"A salamander? Why are . . . ?"

The crashing and crackling was echoed up ahead of them. Then Flash saw one of the creatures. It was nine feet long, a muddy green with splotches of yellow running along its thick glistening body. It opened its wide mouth and Flash saw it was unlike any of the tiny salamanders he was familiar with in ways other than size. It had large snake-like fangs.

With a few more lumbering steps of its four squatty feet, the giant salamander blocked their path completely.

CHAPTER FIVE

Zarkov was grumbling. His broad back was pressed against the black rock wall of a vast cavern and he was complaining. "It must be evening by now," he boomed. "I have an excellent time sense, I'm not usually wrong. It's evening and that's another meal missed." He made an attempt to scratch his ample beard, but the leather cords which bound his wrists prevented him from doing an adequate job.

Several yards across the black cave, a small fire burned, sending sooty smoke up to vanish in the thick shadows. Seated near the fire were three lean men, wearing hooded robes and sandals.

"I've been in captivity on six planets, four satellites, and one lesser moon," continued the bearded scientist in his big voice. "They always made a point of feeding me, especially on Jupiter where they were fattening me up for an impending cannibal feast, which fortunately—"

"You must be patient." One of the robed men stood to face the trussed Zarkov. "These are difficult times on Mongo. Many people do not eat at all. It is especially difficult for us, who are sorcerers and therefore—"

"If you were any kind of sorcerers, you'd magic up a meal."

"Wait until our leader arrives. We will see to all your needs then," promised the hooded sorcerer.

Zarkov had been a prisoner several hours. His flying safety belt had worked perfectly after a brief initial period of uncontrolled plummeting. He had drifted down through the bright day. The controls functioned well and he had been able to aim himself at the road he saw below.

"Look at the size of that *linaria canadensis*," he remarked as he made a bouncing, dust-raising landing on the jungle roadway. The weeds, giant yet delicate, rose up to heights of five and six feet.

Fists on hips, Zarkov surveyed his landing place. "Fascinating," he decided. "Exactly what I expected."

Loosening the flying belt, he shoved one big hand into a pocket of his worksuit and brought out a carob-coated protein square. He was about to pop it into his mouth when he heard something.

A very small sound, but he was certain it had been made by a foot stepping on a dry twig.

Scratching at his bushy beard, Zarkov strode across the road to peer into the high forest. "I've had all kinds of receptions in my forty-odd years," he said to himself, "and, usually, the ones who come sneaking and pussyfooting mean you the least good."

Someone dropped down on his back from the trees above. An arm circled his thick neck, tightening.

"What's this?" roared Zarkov. He swung a fist back, feeling it connect with a nose.

"Nay, Brother Igon, don't damage his brain," cautioned a voice from out of the brush. "We need his impressive intellect."

From the corner of his eye, Zarkov got a glimpse of the man riding his back, and of a metal rod poised to strike. Zarkov dropped backwards, slamming the man into the trunk of a tree.

The man barked out his breath and let go.

The doctor took a step clear but was jumped by two other men. Each was tall and powerful, wearing a hooded robe.

Zarkov got rid of one with a slashing uppercut. The other hooded man held tight.

"This will cause too much damage to us all," said the one called Brother Igon. "Use the flask on him, Brother Beltor."

A cork popped, green fumes spilled into Zarkov's face. He gave one more angry bellow before falling forward into a bush thick with spikey branches.

He had awakened, thoroughly tied at wrist and ankle, in this huge black-walled cave.

Now catching the attention of the one called Brother Beltor, Dr. Zarkov said, "Let me ask you something which has nothing to do with food. When you three grabbed me, something was said about my intelligence, my intellect. Granted I'm one of the more brilliant men in the universe, still it's certain my reputation doesn't extend to Mongo."

"That is true, Dr. Zarkov," replied Brother Beltor. "We believe one with your mental capacities can do much to aid the sorcerers' cause."

"But how did you know for sure I had such mental capacities?"

The lean sorcerer spread out his hands. "We read your mind," he said simply.

CHAPTER SIX

Dale had landed about five minutes before Zarkov, and some ten miles to the East.

Her flying belt had functioned well, carrying her gently down and away from the stricken survey ship. She'd looked up at it for the first minute of her drop, watching it roar away from her, hoping Flash would be able to save the ship. She was concerned about him, but she knew he was capable of surviving even if the craft did crash.

Dale concentrated on controlling her descent. She saw thick jungle stretched out below her in all directions. When she'd dropped another thousand feet she saw a road cutting through the trees and brush, and immediately off the road a circle of clearing with a pool at its center.

"As good a place as any to land."

The dark-haired girl misjudged her course slightly. At the last moment she had to make some hurried corrections on the control buckle to avoid landing in the trees. As it was, she hit into a palm tree at the pool edge, did a wobbly spin in midair and landed with one foot bent beneath her.

"Darn, feels like a sprain." Wincing she turned off the belt, pushed down on the mossy ground with her hands. "No, it's only a bad twist." She found she was still able to walk, though it was painful.

Hoofbeats sounded out on the road, dust came spinning across the clearing, skimming the wide pool.

"Look what's dropped out of the trees, Alex," said the first horseman as he reigned in. He was a large, chunky man, bearded and wearing a black cloak trimmed in gold. On his head was a gold helmet with a scarlet plume fluttering from its crown. Through an opening in the dark cloak, a breastplate of gold armor showed.

"Lovely." Alex was not quite as chunky as his companion, and his gold helmet was plumeless. "A very lovely find, Captain. One hardly expects to come across such a prize in this desolate stretch of the kingdom."

"And was it not you, Alex, who wanted to meet our flying ship further up the river?" The captain laughed, still watching the dark-haired Dale. "Had we taken that course of action, we would have missed this maiden, who will surely be worth a commendation from the emperor himself."

"Perhaps even a promotion for you, Captain."

Dale took an unsteady step ahead. "Who are you?"

The captain, laughing, touched his gloved hand to his gold helmet. "I am Captain Hakes of the Royal Police, at your service, my girl. Accompanying me is my trusted lieutenant, Alex."

Alex, gloved hands on the pommel of his saddle, leaned in the direction of the girl. "You are not from this territory," he said. "Where are you from?"

"I'm part of an exploration team," Dale answered, moving her hand slowly toward the control panel of her flying belt. "We come, originally, from a planet called Earth."

"We?" asked the chunky captain. "Where are the others?"

"There was some trouble with our ship. We had to jump."

"How many of you are there?"

"Three."

"All, as yourself, young girls?"

"No, I'm the only woman on the team."

"Where are the others likely to land?"

Dale hesitated. "I'm not certain."

"Not nearby, apparently," remarked Alex.

"You are indeed fortunate," Captain Hakes told Dale, "to have come under the protection of the Royal Police. Being unfamiliar with our kingdom you do not realize what a dangerous and untamed area you find yourself in. Come along with us now, my girl."

Dale shook her head. "I have to wait for the others," she said. "Here."

"Nonsense. You'll be much more comfortable in the capital," the captain said. "Emperor Ming, by the way, is a man of considerable learning himself. He will be most anxious to talk to you and your friends."

"Particularly you," added Alex, chuckling.

"That sounds very nice," said Dale. "When my friends arrive here at this rendezvous spot, we'll all be happy to accept your invitation."

"No need to wait," insisted the captain. "We can make arrangements for your associates to be met."

"I'd prefer to wait."

Captain Hakes nodded at his lieutenant. "Alex, persuade the young lady to accompany us."

Dale jabbed the rise button on her flying belt.

Captain Hakes swung from his saddle, gave a tremendous leap.

He caught hold of Dale's legs before she had lifted more than four feet off the ground. The two of them hung suspended, neither rising nor falling, swaying in the air.

With a clenched fist, the captain reached up and slammed at the controls.

The belt made a sputtering sound. They both dropped to the ground.

Captain Hakes stood up and away from the fallen girl. "I'd advise you to accept our invitation without any further delay," he told her.

CHAPTER SEVEN

Harn, Flash's guide, cried out in fright, "They will devour us!"

Palm fronds, broken branches, leaves scattered down on them as a second gigantic salamander came thrashing onto the trail.

"This way," said Flash. Escape was still possible to their left.

The bent man took several unsteady steps back from the fanged salamander which cut off their further progress. He gave a frightened look to his side. As he turned to run in the direction Flash had indicated, his foot caught in a twist of shaggy vine.

"I am undone," he cried as he went sprawling across the trail.

The second salamander lowered its head toward the fallen man.

"Ease yourself along flat on the ground," advised Flash. "You can crawl over here."

"My life is at its end, outlander," said Harn, "for I cannot seem to disentangle my foot."

The salamander's head was three feet above the struggling Harn. Its mouth gaped open, showing the curved fangs and a huge split tongue.

Flash reached beneath his tunic. With his blaster pistol in his hand, he took two steps forward. "Keep your head down," he warned Harn.

The pistol sent a sizzling shot at the attacking salamander. There was a faint hollow explosive sound and the head of the giant creature turned to charred dust.

"A miracle," exclaimed Harn. "Great and powerful wizardry!"

The headless salamander thrashed and writhed, crashing into tree trunks and trampling brush. Then it fell dead.

Harn rose up gingerly, tugged his trapped foot clear of the thick twist of vine. "His mate fears us now," he said, laughing his dry laugh.

The other enormous salamander had moved away from them, returning to the safety of the jungle.

After a glance around, Flash put his pistol away in his waistband. "Let's get going again, then."

Harn came closer to him. "That is indeed a powerful weapon, outlander," he said in a whispering voice. "Much more powerful than anything the Royal Police possess." He pointed at the tunic which concealed the gun. "You are wise to conceal it, for to be caught with such a weapon would mean certain death."

"After a pretty good struggle."

Nodding, the guide said, "You need not fear that I will betray you, outlander. For now I owe you my life and there is nothing Harn would not do for you."

"Okay, then take me to the inn," said Flash. "I want to get to the capital as soon as I can."

The bleeding heart, pierced with a silver arrow, showed through the swirling mist.

Harn cocked his head toward the hanging inn sign. "We have arrived safely," he said to Flash. "All thanks to the gods that we did. Truly, had you not used your—"

"I don't think," Flash cut in, "it will be a good idea to talk about our meeting with the salamanders any further."

"Aye," agreed Harn. "You are absolutely right, outlander." He began climbing the brick steps leading to the oaken door of the sprawling shingled inn. "For while you may trust Harn, there is no telling what others may do. All live in fear of Ming the Merciless in these times."

Light and warmth spilled out of the opened doorway. The room they entered was large, with a beamed ceiling and a big stone fireplace. There were a dozen round wooden tables around the room, a long serving bar against the near wall.

Two wide men in dark tunics and hightop muddy boots sat at a table hunched over copper tankards of ale. One of the men wore a scarlet headband and had a single loop of silver dangling from his left ear.

There were no other patrons in the Heart & Arrow Inn. Behind the bar, giving most of his attention to tapping a fresh keg of ale, was the proprietor. He was fat, with a striped apron tied around his flabby waist. He wore a leather vest which concealed only part of his hairy ballooning torso. "Ah, good evening to you, Harn," he said as he glanced their way.

"We wish a private dining room." Harn trotted toward the bar. "My friend has traveled a good long way, from a far-off territory. He's worn and hungry, Blessing." He lowered his voice. "Later we would appreciate a small discussion with you."

Fat Blessing said, "Take any room you fancy, Harn. As you can observe, we are not doing a thriving business this night." He leaned an enormous elbow on the bar top, tilting his shaggy bulk in Flash's direction. "Whereabout do you hail from, sir?"

"A long way off," Flash replied.

"Ah, you wish to be discreet," said the innkeeper. "You'll find the Heart & Arrow's a place which respects a man's privacy."

Drumming his fingers slowly on the bar, Harn said, "I think we must celebrate my friend's safe arrival.

Do you have any of your special brandy left in stock, Blessing?"

The innkeeper's left eyelid fluttered for an instant. "The special brandy, did you say . . . aye, that I do, Harn. As the gods would have it, a new supply has found its way to me this very day." He gave Flash a jiggling smile. "You must understand, sir, that this particular brandy is of such quality that our emperor would prefer to have the entire supply find its way to the palace. However, now and again, a bottle or two reaches me by way of the Great River."

"Ale will be sufficient for me," said Flash.

"Oh, nay," insisted Harn. "I owe you a good deal, my friend, and you must allow me to make this grateful gesture."

Flash grinned. "Very well."

"We will dine in that room beyond the fireplace," Harn told the fat innkeeper. "When you have the brandy ready, serve it there if you will."

"You realize, sir," Blessing confided to Flash, "I must keep such a rare drink well hidden. You will excuse me while I fetch it."

The small dining room had whitewashed plaster walls, a beamed ceiling and a good-sized fireplace of its own.

"I'll fix things so we can warm ourselves, outlander," said Harn as he shuffled to the fireplace. Kneeling, he put a wax match to the kindling beneath the crossed logs. "There, it will soon be blazing heartily."

"Hem," coughed Blessing from the doorway. "Here is the brandy. You will find, sir, it compares favorably with the best you have ever sampled."

"Of that I'm sure," Flash replied, taking one of the glasses from the tray the fat man held out toward him.

Harn took the remaining glass, sniffing at it. "Ah, a wonderful scent to it."

"I will send a girl soon to take your order," said Blessing as he withdrew and shut the door.

"Well," said Flash, raising his glass toward the guide, "cheers."

Harn hesitated, rubbed at his stomach. "You must forgive me, outlander." Glass in hand, he backed unsteadily into a rough-hewn chair beside the wooden dining table. "The shock of our recent brush with death has just caught up with me . . . I feel I must sit quietly for a moment or two."

"Brandy's exactly what you need to snap you out of your funk, Harn."

"I don't believe I can hold anything in my stomach at the moment, my friend. Please, though, you go ahead and enjoy your brandy."

"Very well then." Flash turned to look into the now crackling fire. When he turned again to face Harn, the glass was empty. "You were right. It's an excellent . . ."

Harn, poised on the edge of his chair, watched him. "What is wrong, outlander?"

"I . . . don't . . . I don't . . ." Flash swung one hand out. He dropped to his knees, then toppled over on his side and lay still.

CHAPTER EIGHT

"I don't think we dare risk it," the huge innkeeper was saying. He sat, his thick legs spread wide, on a chair near the fireplace in the small dining room.

"There's no risk, I'm telling you." Harn paced the wooden floor, carefully avoiding the still-sprawled Flash. "I've had much practice deceiving Captain Hakes."

"Aye, but the captain surely knows this outlander must have a weapon of an exceptional sort," said Blessing. "You told me yourself they found one on the girl's person while they were tying her."

"The captain, surely, will expect the blond outlander to have a similar weapon," admitted Harn. "However, I will simply tell him of our struggle with the salamanders. The stranger's pistol was lost during that fearsome encounter." He gave one of his dry rattling laughs. "So anxious was I to deliver this fellow to him that I have not had a chance to return to search for the missing gun."

When Blessing shrugged, ripples ran up and down his fat chest and stomach. "It might work, Harn. Yet—"

"It will work," asserted the bent man. "We will keep the pistol I saw him thrust in his waist. In fact, before we take him down to the wharf we will search his knapsack."

"Wait now, Harn. One pistol we might perhaps keep, but no more."

Harn laughed again, tapping his gnarled fingers

against his chest. Beneath his tunic coins jingled. "So far, Blessing, I have been paid a mere fifty mingots for entrapping this outlander. Yet it has required considerable effort. I had to wait long dreary hours in the jungle, I had to use my nimble wits to invent a plausible tale with which to lure him here. I have even risked death. That, you must admit, is worth a good deal more than fifty mingots."

"You will receive another fifty when you deliver him to the Royal Police airship which is going to meet you at the wharf," pointed out the fat innkeeper. "Don't forget, by the way, I am to get a cut for my assistance."

"Yes, yes," said Harn, brushing aside Blessing's last remark with his hand. "Think of the pistol, though, Blessing. It is far more effective, I assure you, than anything the Royal Police or the Imperial Army have." He crossed to the fire, held his hands out to it. "There's no calculating what price it might bring in certain quarters. I am sure the sorcerers would like to bid on it, and most certainly the lion men."

"Lion men," snorted Blessing. "Threadbare rebels who live like savages in the wilds and dream of the overthrow of Ming. Why, they could not afford the price of a dinner at the Heart & Arrow, let alone something such as that pistol."

"You forget that during a war men tell lies," said Harn. "It is known as propaganda. The lion men have supporters, you may be sure, supporters who can more than afford to buy the outlander's pistol from us." He rubbed his warmed palms together. "There is also Prince Barin himself."

The fat innkeeper shook his head. "He and his followers are still cowering in the Forest Kingdom, Harn, fearful of the wrath of Ming."

"Perhaps. Or perhaps that, too, is merely propaganda," said Harn. "At any rate, I will take his pistol now. For I have but little time to hide it safely before we carry this outlander down to the wharf."

"He's going to be heavy, I wager," said Blessing. "Lately, whenever I lift anything heavy, I get this frightful pain all across—"

"Let me save you the trouble then," said Flash, bounding to his feet. "And here, Harn, is the pistol you're so anxious about." He pointed the weapon at the approaching guide.

"What does this mean?" muttered Blessing.

"It means, you blubbery fool," cried Harn, "the knockout potion you put in his drink was not strong enough."

"Not at all." Flashed grinned. "It means I poured the brandy into the fireplace and only pretended to be unconscious. I had an uncle, back on the planet Earth, who warned me never to drink with strangers. Now then, Harn, the money."

"What are you alluding to, outlander?"

"The coins you were rattling a moment ago. I'm going to need some local spending money. Hand them over."

"I'm afraid you misunder—"

"Five more seconds and I'll take them off your corpse," Flash told him. He had no intention of killing the man, but he knew such a bluff would work with Harn.

"Very well, if you would rob a man of the fruits of his toil." Harn slid a hand into his tunic.

"If anything but money comes out, Harn, that means you're dead, too."

"They are in a pouch of leather, outlander, given to me by my careworn grandmother on her—"

"The money."

Slowly Harn handed the pouch to Flash. "You surely have no chance, outlander. The Royal Police know the young woman had two men with her. They will not rest until they have the both of you."

"As of now, they only have the girl?"

"So I have been led to believe."

"And she is in the capital?"

"Aye, where you also will soon be," said Harn. "Only you will be in a cell deep underground and she—"

"Blessing—" interrupted Flash.

"I did only as I was bidden, sir. There's really no need to kill me."

Flash reached back into his rucksack, brought out a small coil of plastic rope. "Tie up your friend here."

"Nay, he's no friend of mine," Blessing said. Why, I barely know the fellow."

"Tie him up and gag him well," ordered Flash. "Then I'll do the same for you. Be quick about it. I have an appointment with the Royal Police."

CHAPTER NINE

The man in the high tower stood watching the vast city spread out below in the darkness. A city of towers, spires, minarets, and pennants, illuminated with hundreds of floating globes of pastel light. "I often think," he observed, "that the people of Mongo are singularly lacking in gratitude." He gestured at the huge window with a spidery hand. "I give them such a lovely gracious capital for their empire and yet . . ." He sighed, crossed the circular room to a round highly polished table to pick up several sheets of flimsy paper. "The spirit of rebellion and dissatisfaction continues on the rise." He dropped into a high-back throne-like chair on a dais next to the table, steepled his fingers in front of his lean sharp-featured face. "I'm afraid there's nothing to do but increase the public executions."

Seated in a lower chair was a burly man with close-cropped hair, the Minister of Police. "A wise remedy, Ming," he said, "though perhaps at this time . . . We are approaching the harvest season and, as you know, there is already a serious food—"

"I also feel my people are lacking in basic intelligence," interrupted Ming. "My recent proclamation gave them several excellent solutions to this alleged famine. Yet they persist in agitating and ignoring my advice." He was a long gaunt man of fifty, dressed in a jeweled saffron robe. He wore a peaked skull cap on his hairless head and had a down-curving moustache and the wisp of a goatee. He stroked this tiny beard now. "If they ignore sound imperial wisdom, Erik, then they must suffer the consequences. We will have five additional public executions a week. One from each of the five most complaining territories."

"Very well, sir," said the burly Erik.

A younger man, wearing clothes of a slightly military cut, was slouched against one of the arches next to a window. "Seems to me we ought to revive the tournaments," he said.

Ming turned his gaunt face toward the young man. "As Minister of Agriculture, Haldor, you needn't involve yourself with public entertainments."

"Even so," said Haldor with a smile, "I think the tournaments would be very useful about now."

Ming leaned forward on his throne chair, placing one hand on his knee. "How so?"

"Main thing is, they take the people's minds off their other problems," said the young minister. "You've got a lot of dissatisfied citizens right here in the capital, you know. Important people, many of them, people whose support, especially financial, we need. And when people like that start worrying about their food supply, you're—"

"There is no food shortage in the capital," said Ming sharply. "If certain fools and buffoons believe so it is because you, Haldor, have not done an adequate job of explaining the agricultural situation to them."

"Maybe," answered Haldor, still smiling. "Anyway, Ming, about the tournaments. We could round up most of the best known troublemakers in each territory. Toss them in the arena with various wild animals, possibly even a few apemen and . . ."

"What are the advantages of all that?" asked Erik.

"The main thing is, we get rid of a good lot of people who are against the present empire," explained

Haldor. "But with the tournaments, we don't do it as obviously as with public executions."

Ming sighed once again. "You give them credit for far more maturity than they have, Haldor," he said. "Nonetheless, I think we might introduce a new series of tournaments. That will be, however, in addition to the increased number of public executions. Attend to the details, Erik, and I will issue a proclamation."

"Very well, sir."

Ming rested his chin on the sharp tips of his steepled fingers. "Yes, a touch of pageantry always goes over well, takes their minds off their fancied troubles," he said. "Princess Aura will need a new wardrobe for attending the tournaments." He glanced down at Erik. "Where is my daughter, by the way?"

"Well . . ." Erik stretched out the word, but couldn't come up with anything to follow it.

Haldor laughed. "She's out practicing democracy."

Ming frowned. "What do you mean?"

"I mean Princess Aura slipped out of the palace this afternoon, dressed as a commoner," replied the minister. "She enjoys getting out among the people to find out—"

"Find out they're a pack of fools," said the emperor angrily. "I've forbidden Aura to do such foolish things. Erik, have her found and returned to the palace at once."

"My men are already scouring the city for the princess, sir," replied the burly Minister of Police.

Haldor waited a second before saying, "We have much bigger problems."

Ming said, "You derive too much amusement from your present position. Perhaps you would be more serious in a lower one."

"Perhaps." The smile remained on the young man's face. "At any rate, I think we should be giving more attention to the fact that three people from some alien planet have apparently landed on Mongo."

"*Apparently* is the key word," the emperor said. "I have a full report on the alleged incident here." He rattled the papers in his hand.

"We have men scouring the jungle to locate these supposed aliens," said Erik, "and to find their ship. As of now, we have only the girl."

"Which reminds me," said Ming, rising. "I promised Captain Hakes I would join him in the interrogation of the young woman."

"She's rumored to be quite pretty," remarked Haldor.

"Pretty or not," said Ming, "we'll find out soon enough if there is any truth to her story."

"Suppose there is?"

"I shouldn't have to remind you, Haldor, that we have been invincible so far," Ming told him. "We shall continue to be. There is no one, be he from Mongo or some distant planet, whom the power of Ming cannot subdue." He strode toward an arched exit. "You would do well to remember that."

The lean sorcerer came toward Zarkov with a knife in his hand.

The burly scientist, who'd been dozing against the cave wall, blinked awake. "Decided to do me in after all, have you?"

"No need to boom so, Dr. Zarkov," said Brother Beltor. "My companions are trying to sleep. I am only going to cut loose your bonds."

"Highly wasteful," commented Zarkov, in a slightly less booming voice. "Untie the knots, then you can reuse the rope."

"I am no good at all with knots," apologized the sorcerer. "Brother Anmar will be here soon and you'll be dining with him."

"If he brings any chow," added Zarkov.

"He has provisions, no need to worry." Beltor began slicing the ropes.

"You can communicate mind to mind?"

"Yes. We worked out the basic principles before Ming banished us."

"Ming would be who?"

"The emperor of the New Kingdom," explained Beltor. "After successfully overthrowing and conquering the legitimate governments of this area he outlawed those of us who wouldn't work for him."

When Zarkov's hands were free, he used them to smooth out his tangled black beard. "This Ming fellow uses magic and sorcery to run his empire?"

Finishing his job, Beltor stepped back. "We were not always sorcerers."

"You must forgive Beltor. He sometimes overdoes the mystifying element in our guise." A tall light-haired man of forty had entered the cave. He wore a robe similar to the other sorcerers, hood back off his head. Throwing down a rough cloth sack of supplies, he said, "I hope you don't mind dining on thram."

"At this point, I'll eat most anything," said Zarkov. "Even thram, whatever it may be."

"It's much like your Earth . . . rabbit," said the blond man.

"Read that off my brain, huh?"

He extended his hand. "Yes. I am Brother Anmar," he said. "I'm happy to have a man of your intellect among us, Dr. Zarkov."

"So happy that you're not going to let me go?"

"I'm afraid for the moment we must keep you with us," said Anmar. "There is a particular problem we need a solution to, and you seem qualified to lend a hand. In the morning, then, we will begin our journey to the Forest Kingdom."

"What sort of problem?"

"It involves a weapon, a new type of blaster cannon for aircraft, which is not turning out as expected."

"Weapons are right up my alley," said Zarkov in his resounding voice. "I almost majored in weaponry back at the London Institute of Technology."

Brother Beltor took up the supply sack, carried it toward the sooty fire. "I'll begin to prepare the meal."

Zarkov grunted to his feet, brushing at the legs of his worksuit. "I didn't come to your blasted Mongo alone," he said. "Have you plucked that fact out of my head yet?"

"Yes, I know about Dale Arden and Flash Gordon," replied the chief sorcerer. "I am sorry we can't spare you yet to search for them."

"Do you know if they're alive and kicking, and where they might be?" Zarkov asked.

Anmar gave a negative shake of his head. "We haven't devised an attachment yet allowing us to tap the particular extrasensory ability needed to find out such information."

"Attachment?" bellowed the doctor. "You've been trying to con me, is that it? You're not magicians at all, you're—"

"Exactly," said Anmar. "Scientists."

CHAPTER TEN

A dozen wooden docks extended from the riverside, their far ends lost in the thick fog which hung over the river. The road leading downhill toward the wharf area was made of cobblestones, slick and black in the misty night. A small settlement had grown up at this spot on the Great River, about twenty low buildings of wood and stone, clustered randomly along the shore. Narrow lanes, some paved with stones, others merely twisting paths of mud, ran through the ramshackle town.

Flash moved slowly through the foggy streets. Round his shoulders was the dark cloak he had borrowed from the now bound and gagged Harn. "Shouldn't be too difficult to spot an airship around here," Flash said to himself.

It was his intention to commandeer the police craft, use it to fly somewhere near the capital. Then he would take Dale away from the Emperor Ming. But before he could work out the details of that rescue, he would have to get a look at the emperor's city.

From some of the windows of the wharf town came fuzzy yellow light. And out of one ramshackle building, smoke and noise and gruff laughter came tumbling. A crude sign nailed unevenly over the door announced this was the One-Eyed Mariner Cafe.

A moment after Flash passed its wide open doorway, someone came flying out into the night to land with a huge thumping splash in the muddy lane.

"We may not love Ming here," shouted an angry

voice from the cafe, "but we'll have none of your revolutionary talk."

"More's the pity," replied the man who'd been thrown to the street. "Perhaps you didn't quite comprehend—"

"He needs more of a lesson, I'm thinking," cried another rough voice.

"Let's teach him a good one, the shaggy rogue."

Flash had turned to watch. The man on the ground was big and broad, wearing a leather tunic and a short kilt-like garment instead of trousers. He had a great mane of yellow hair, a thick beard to match. And, it showed swishing as he stood, a three-foot long tail with a tuft of yellow fur at its tip.

"Come on then," challenged the lion man. "Let us see how you fare against Tun."

A large man with a spikey black beard said, "You've got no fight in you, you overgrown tabby." Shoulders hunched, he came stalking toward Tun the lion man.

But another man had materialized out of the swirling fog. He was moving silently toward the lion man's back, carrying in his hand a short wooden club.

"Behind you," warned Flash.

Without turning, the lion man dropped to his knees. His tail slapped at his unseen assailant as the man's swung club hit nothing but air.

Before Tun could rise, the black-bearded man leaped atop him. Another man ran from the inn to join the struggling pile.

The man who'd tried to club Tun reached through the laces of his loose-fitting tunic and drew out a knife.

"No, you don't." Flash's right hand chopped down.

"Hey!" The knife dropped to the mud. The man swung a blow at Flash.

Grinning, Flash sidestepped, catching the fist. He

sent the man spinning away and the fog swallowed him.

One more big man, this one with a soiled black patch over one eye, hurtled out of the cafe and piled on. The three of them were pummeling the roaring lion man.

"Even the three of you can't keep me down," roared Tun. "I'm a better man than the lot of you." He jabbed a fist into the chest of the one with the spikey beard.

"You're no man at all. You're but one step from going on all fours," came the reply.

As much as he wanted to get on and find the airship, Flash stayed.

He bounded to the struggling mound of men. "This isn't a fair contest," he said as he grabbed hold of the man with the eye patch. "If you're the One-Eyed Mariner himself, you'd better attend to business." He yanked the big man free of the tangle, sent him stumbling toward the hazy doorway of the inn.

"Much obliged," gasped Tun. "I can handle these other two on my . . . oof."

A hand shoved his face down into the mud.

Flash caught another man by the shoulders. He set him cartwheeling into the fog. Seconds later, there was the sound of a body breaking through rotten wood. A great splash followed.

"Might as well get rid of this last one," said Flash. He reached out toward the bearded man who was slamming Tun's shaggy head against the ground.

Then something hit Flash behind the ear. Hit him hard twice, then once again.

The fog thickened and thickened, incredibly fast. Then everything turned a glaring black and Flash fell.

CHAPTER ELEVEN

Thin morning sunlight came through the single porthole. Flash sat up on the rough wooden flooring and looked around. He was in a small cabin in some kind of ship, and the ship was moving along the river. He could feel that.

Slumped on the floor just beneath the porthole was Tun. His mouth slightly open, he was soring loudly. There was no furniture in the room, nothing at all.

Flash got himself upright. As he rubbed at the lump behind his ear, he said, "I didn't hear that one coming at all." He crossed, a bit unsteady, to the cabin's thick door. It was locked from the outside.

"Good morning, comrade," said Tun, wakening. Yawning, he stretched his arms up. His tail brushed at the floor. "I sincerely believe I could have beaten that trio of rascals. And, with the help of a fine lad such as yourself, it should have been child's play."

"There were more than three," said Flash, grinning. "It was one of the extra ones who got the jump on me."

The lion man was running his big hands over himself. "I don't seem to have any more welts and lumps than I did when I started. No, wait, here's a nice fresh goose egg on my skull. Well, they put one over on Tun this time." With a grunt, he rose up off the floor. "That's who I am—Tun. My people are called the lion men, a proud and fierce race—as you've no doubt guessed." He held out his hand.

Shaking it, Flash said, "I'm Flash Gordon."

The lion man studied him for a moment. "I've not exactly seen your like before, Flash. Where are you from?"

"From a planet called Earth," replied Flash. He explained his mission to Tun, told him of the crash of the survey ship and of his subsequent search for Dr. Zarkov and Dale.

"Another planet, eh?" Tun rubbed his knuckles over his tangled mane of yellow hair. "How do men live there—is there more freedom?"

"In some places," said Flash. "In my country at present."

"Have you anyone like Ming the Merciless to contend with?"

"Not right now."

"I feel," said Tun, "as do all my people, that Ming must be stopped. Nay, not only stopped but overthrown. He must conquer no further territories; he must be toppled from the rule of those he has already taken."

"How many ways are there of doing that?"

"One," answered the lion man.

"Revolution?"

"Aye." Tun nodded his shaggy head. "Ming, you see, has abolished all general elections and declared himself perpetual ruler of all Mongo. He has closed down the higher courts, making himself the final judge. There is still a parliament, but they are all his puppets and lackeys."

"How did he come to power?"

"There was a long period of depression and famine, much dissatisfaction. The old regime grew weak and Ming staged a coup. From then on, he has been in control of the capital," explained the lion man. "He has built up a huge and ruthless army, a monumental police force."

"To bring off a revolution," said Flash, "you need several things. Not the least of which is weapons."

"Aye, it is now a crime for any but Ming's minions to possess any sort of sophisticated weapon."

Flash remembered his own blaster pistol. He felt under his tunic. The gun was gone. His rucksack had been taken from him as well. "Do you have any idea, Tun, who it is holding us?"

The lion man's tail flicked back and forth. "From the sluggish nature of our progress downriver, I'd guess we're on a barge. A good many of the Great River bargemen transport things which are not strictly legal."

"What do they have in mind for us?"

"I fear we've been grabbed for the purpose of being taken, by way of one of the subsidiary rivers, to a disreputable port town. There we'll likely be sold to slavers."

Flash nodded. "Are we traveling in the direction of the capital?"

"Aye," said Tun with a glance at the porthole.

"Good," said Flash. "We'll have to see about escaping."

Tun lowered his eyes, his tail curled around his leg. "I have to admit a fondness for green ale," he said. "Nothing wrong in that itself, save that it, in my unfortunate case, makes me even more talkative than I normally am. I'll give you a good piece of advice, Flash. Never get into a political discussion in a low waterfront dive."

"Or out in front of one."

"What I'm trying to say is I'm truly sorry an upstanding lad such as yourself got dragged into this mess simply because I couldn't control my tongue. If I . . . "

The heavy door creaked open.

The man on the threshold was incomplete. He had

one leg missing, his left, and one arm gone, his right. He wore wide-bottom trousers, a heavy coat with brass buttons running up the front in two rows. "You," he said, pointing at Flash with his only hand.

Flash watched the man, saying nothing.

"Up above," said the incomplete man.

"Somebody wants to see me on deck?"

"Aye." He took a swaying step backwards. "Come along."

"What about Tun?" asked Tun. "Have you no requests for my company?"

The one armed man flicked his wrist and a long knife appeared in his hand. "Stay here."

Flash stepped out of the cabin. "Who am I going to see?"

"Captain."

"About what?"

"Business," the man answered.

The road was dusty, cutting through dry ruined fields. Already at this early hour, the air was hot and the sun a glaring yellow. The hooves of their horses stirred up swirling spouts of dust.

Zarkov wiped the back of his fist across his mouth. He, too, was now wearing a hooded robe. In the field to his right, he noticed what he at first assumed was a scarecrow. Not an effective one, however, since a cluster of bright green crows were pecking at it, dancing on its arms and head. Then the doctor realized, "It's a man."

Riding beside him, on a roan mare, Brother Anmar said, "Executed at Ming's orders."

"For what reason?"

"His crops failed," said Anmar. "As did many in this valley."

"Do you know the reason for the failure?"

"Oh, yes. The particular kind of war gas which

Ming's airships dropped on the nearby towns and villages killed most of the growing things in this part of the territory."

"Ming won't accept such an excuse?"

"I imagine he does now," said Anmar. "There have been fewer executions of farmers of late. This man, as you no doubt noticed, has been dead several months."

"Will no one cut him down from those poles?"

"That would mean death for whoever did it," answered the blond sorcerer. "If the Royal Police were unable to find the man who did it, they would pick one at random and execute him."

Smoothing his beard, brushing dust from it, Zarkov observed in his loud voice, "No way to run a planet."

Up ahead Brother Beltor looked back over his shoulder. "Perhaps you will be more willing to help us now."

Zarkov's left eye narrowed, new wrinkles gathered on his forehead. "I'd like to see this Ming tossed out," he admitted.

"Such is our objective," said Anmar.

By the side of the road stood two naked boys. The tallest of the two, who was about seven years old, wore a dirty piece of cloth as a patch over his left eye. Each boy held a wooden bowl in scratched, dirty hands.

"Any food, any coins?" they asked.

Brother Igon, who was in the lead, reined up. "You beg a long way from anything." He reached into the knapsack on his saddle.

"We do not wish to risk the town today, sir," said the boy with the eyepatch.

Leaning down, Brother Beltor handed them two silver coins. "Why is that?"

"Five men are to be hanged at midday," explained the other boy.

"For what crime?" asked Igon.

"Not for any crime, sir," said the boy. "Merely as an example to us all."

"We have seen more than enough such examples," added the one-eyed boy. "Thus, we have come away from the town today to try our luck here."

"Well, here is some bread and cheese for you," said Igon.

"Thank you, sir."

The five horsemen rode on.

Zarkov looked back twice at the thin naked boys. After a few moments of silent riding he asked, "These public executions are held often?"

"Very often," replied Anmar. "Each week ofttimes, in many of our towns and villages. It is intended to keep the people docile and fearful of Ming. As you may imagine, it frequently has the opposite effect."

"Are we traveling as far as the next town by horseback?"

"Aye, we still have several miles to travel ere we reach the concealed airship which is to carry us to the Forest Kingdom."

"Will we reach the town before midday?"

"We should."

"Dressed as wandering conjurers," said the burly doctor, "we can pass through the town?"

"Aye, as I explained last night. In many parts of our planet, there is still a belief in witchcraft and magic," said Anmar. "Even those who do not believe enjoy witnessing a few mystifying tricks now and again. Thus, we pretend to be sorcerers and, so far, Ming has not harmed any of our ranks. We are able to move freely across the land. Though should the emperor learn the real identity of any of us, he would be swift to act."

"Doesn't anybody ever try to stop these executions?" Zarkov asked.

"It would mean death for any who dared try."

Zarkov rubbed his hand across his middle. Beneath his robe his blaster was tucked in a pocket of his worksuit. Anmar, putting him on his honor, had returned the weapon before they had begun their day's journey. "Not necessarily," he said.

"What do you mean?"

Zarkov said nothing more.

CHAPTER TWELVE

The captain was crouched in the bow of the barge, with Flash's rucksack on the deck at his feet. He was a round-shouldered man with a scarlet kerchief tied round his head. "Perhaps you and I can come to terms which will prove satisfactory to both of us," he said in a low throaty voice.

Flash stood at the starboard rail, studying the countryside they were passing through. It was all thick foliage, growing right down to the river edge. Great twisted roots tangled in the water, splotched with a yellow-green moss. "What do you have in mind?"

"I don't wish to display this certain item out in the open here."

"Let's talk in your cabin then."

"That's worse," said the captain. "Whilst they can't always see what I am up to, they can hear better. No, this is the best spot for a confidential chat." He squatted down lower, tapping the rucksack with his knee. "I put the one which was taken from you in here with the others. Too many have seen it as it is."

Flash turned to face him. "So you're interested in the guns?"

The man's weathered face puckered. "Don't go bawling it about in the breeze," he cautioned. "We must be careful. Such items are, as you well know, forbidden. Were I to be found with these I'd be hanging by the neck in some public square before nightfall. Aye, it's a great risk that I'm taking."

"Maybe you ought to turn them over to the Royal Police."

The captain's face grew more wrinkled. "No, that is not exactly what I had in mind," he said. "What I have been thinking on is this. How did you come by these items?"

Flash watched him for a few seconds. "You'd like more, is that it?"

"Aye." His head bobbed up and down. "Even these three—why, they would bring a fortune if sold in the right place. Granted I am no expert, yet they look to me to be of the highest craftsmanship. These seem far better than anything the Royal Police have. I imagine you represent some clandestine manufacturer."

Flash said, "Who would you sell them to?"

"You must know the likely customers as well as I do," said the captain with a frown. "You, a man who'd risk smuggling this kind of thing, must know exactly who is in the market for such merchandise."

"I'm interested in your views of the market."

"Well, sir, for the quickest money I would go to the pirate bands to the south of here," the captain said thoughtfully. "Though they will not pay near as much as Prince Barin."

"Prince Barin," repeated Flash. He had heard Harn and the innkeeper talk of the man.

"It is true that you can come by more of these?" His knobby hand stroked the sack which held Flash's blaster pistols.

Flash lowered himself until he was looking the captain in the eye. "I'm not sure I can trust you."

"Ask any man on the river," said the captain, his voice rising. "I have been a bargeman since I was a whey-faced lad. There's no man living who dares call Captain Norlag dishonest."

Grinning, Flash said, "Yet I have the notion you were planning to sell me to the slavers."

"Eh?" Captain Norlag looked away, tugging at the knot of his head scarf. After clearing his throat, he leaned closer to Flash. "I'll be completely frank with you, sir. I did intend perhaps to see what they would offer me for your companion. These are lean times, you must know, and lion men, despite their surly ways, are good workers. They usually fetch a handsome price. You, however, sir, I never considered selling to any—"

"Are you planning to continue toward the capital?"

The captain hesitated. "Well, yes," he said finally. "We have a consignment to pick up twenty miles further down river."

"Let me discuss the situation with my companion."

"Do you mean to tell me that nappy rogue is a partner of yours, sir?"

"He has to be part of any deal I make with you," answered Flash. "He'll help me decide whether the people I represent will wish to do business with you."

Norlag said, "Very well, so be it. How many of these, uh, items do you think you might be able to provide me with?"

"How many can you sell?"

He sucked in his breath. "Are you saying, sir, there is no limit to the quantity?"

"If I can get you one, I can get you a dozen."

"A dozen? May the gods bless me! Why, with a dozen of these, a man . . ." He gave a throaty chuckle.

"Now as to price," said Flash.

"Well, sir, you must realize that I'm to be taking all the risks. Suppose I were to offer you twenty percent of whatever I make?"

"No, we usually get at least sixty," said Flash. "Though perhaps I can talk them into accepting fifty percent."

"Fifty?" The captain slapped his rough hand against his forehead.

"You won't get weapons like this from anyone else on Mongo."

After a few thoughtful snorts through his broad nose, the captain said, "Very well, sir, we shall call it fifty. Here is the hand of Captain Norlag on it."

When Flash returned to the little cabin below deck, the lion man asked him, "What transpired twixt you and our worthy captain?"

Flash said, "I think if I can keep bluffing him for a while longer, we won't get sold to the slavers."

There were banners flying in the town square, musicians in crimson cloaks played festive tunes, vendors sold bright novelties, and there was even a little food to be had. But the people stood silent on the rose-colored cobblestones of the square. Thin, threadbare people. They made no pretense of enjoying themselves. Here and there a highly polished Royal Policeman laughed and joked, but none of that rang quite true. By a half hour before the scheduled time for the executions, even the police had grown silent. All around the high wooden gallows silence reigned.

Dr. Zarkov had a good view of everything. He was stretched out on the flat stone roof of a two-story inn across the square from the wide scaffold. He was dressed again in his worksuit, so as not to connect the sorcerers with what he planned to do. In his hand, he held his pistol.

Beside him, wearing now a farmer's guise, was Brother Anmar. "I still have grave misgivings," he whispered.

"You can ride out and wait for me beyond the town, as the others have done," said Zarkov softly. When necessary, he could talk in a whisper.

"No, when you outlined your idea I told you I would help you," said Anmar, "though I am beginning to regret having given you permission to try this. You are a very persuasive fellow. Yet we don't want to lose a mind such as yours."

"I guarantee you," said Zarkov in a louder whisper, "that I will be using my brain for quite a while to come. Ming and his bully boys aren't going to be dangling Zarkov at the end of a rope in the foreseeable future." He inched forward frowning. "Let's see now. They've got the prisoners in that gray stone building down there, to the rear of the gallows."

"Yes, with five policemen guarding it on the outside."

Zarkov shrugged. "Three in front and two in back," he said. "So if we hit the back side of the place we've got only two to worry about right off the bat." He scrutinized the town square further. "They seem to have just one airship as far as I can tell. That's it there in the courtyard to the rear of the jailhouse." He rubbed at his bearded chin. "Simplest thing is to put the ship out of commission. Could use it for the prisoners to get away in, but it might take too long for me to show them how to use the damn thing."

"You know how to operate a type of airship you've never seen before?"

"Don't see why not," answered Zarkov. "Now, where are their horses? Ah, yes, in that stable off to the side of the jailhouse. And what's that parked near the mouth of the street we want to use—a hay wagon, isn't it? Good." The doctor, in a low crouch, began working his way back across the roof.

He swung over the edge away from the square, let go, and dropped down to a second floor balcony. The small balcony groaned when Zarkov's bulk hit it. He leaped from there to catch hold of a clay drain pipe. On the stones of the alley, he waited for Anmar to make a similar descent.

"Remind me to give you a list of exercises that'll

limber you up," said Zarkov when the sorcerer was beside him. "Ten minutes a day, guaranteed to work."

"My schedule at present leaves little time for recreation," Anmar replied, after catching his breath.

Zarkov concealed his pistol again in a side pocket. "Let's get going."

Sticking to the alleys and sidestreets he'd checked out from above, the doctor led Anmar around to a position near the rear of the jailhouse. The street he'd chosen for an escape route was empty, most of its shops and houses closed up.

"Now for a small distraction." Zarkov withdrew a short red cylindrical object from another pocket. "You get over behind the hay wagon, brother. When we come galloping by, you give it a hefty shove to block the road for a bit."

"We?"

"Me and the prisoners," said Zarkov. "Are you in good enough shape to get the wagon rolling?"

"You've nothing to fear on that score."

"If I can't swipe an extra horse for you, you'll have to ride tandem with me. We shall see." So saying, Zarkov left the sorcerer to edge along the empty street.

One of the police guards was leaning with his hips against the wrought-iron stair rail which led up to the rear door of the jail. The other, hardly more than a boy, was pacing a few yards in front of the snub-nosed police airship.

When the boy turned toward the other guard, Zarkov ran zigzagging for the ship. He made it and jumped up on the wing. The body of the ship hid him now from the two Royal Police.

He lit the rescue flare he'd been clutching in his hand and tossed it beneath the ship.

Ten seconds later, an enormous hissing began. Red

and yellow sparks started to spurt out wildly from under the craft.

"By all the gods," exclaimed the young guard. "What's wrong?" He trotted up to the ship, tugged out his keys and opened the cockpit door. "What should I turn off?"

"Excuse me, young fellow." Zarkov gave him a careful chop to the neck and the boy slumped. The nose of the ship still masked his doings.

Shoving the unconscious guard up into the aircraft, Zarkov climbed in. After a swift survey of the controls, he said, "Simple. Extremely simple." He laughed, snapping his big fingers. "Ah, we'll take care of a couple birds with one stone."

He activated the ship and ran it smack into the rear wall of the jail.

The other guard, who had been watching the ship and the profusion of sparks, was able to throw himself off the stairs just before impact.

The blunt nose of the police ship made a sizable hole in the backside of the jailhouse. An instant after the crash, Zarkov was out of the aircraft and scurrying through the hole.

A puzzled, wide-eyed sergeant, staring at the fresh debris and trying to put on his gold helmet, didn't notice Zarkov until the burly scientist was a foot in front of him. "What means . . . ?"

Zarkov knocked him out. There was a ring with two dozen keys at the man's belt. "No time for that," decided Zarkov.

He darted down a corridor and located the cell area. "Stand back from the door, gents," he told the five prisoners.

The blaster crackled, the cell door disappeared.

"Okay," Zarkov told them," everybody out into the stableyard. Pick a mount and hightail it down the street. Head out of town."

"Do you really think," asked one of the prisoners, "we have a chance to gain our freedom?"

"I guarantee it," bellowed Zarkov. "Now get moving. I have to revive the sergeant and tell him a little something."

CHAPTER THIRTEEN

The attack came a few minutes after sunset.

By day's end, the barge was moving through a swampy stretch of land. Mist rose up between the trunks of the dark trees on both sides of the narrowing river. There was only a deadly jungle silence outside.

"I should never have left the hot dry climate where we lion men are meant to live." Tun was looking through the porthole. "And wherefore did I, you may well ask. It was in order to attempt to raise . . . hey!"

Flash crossed to him. "What is it?"

The shaggy man stuck his head further out into the growing darkness. His long tail swept to and fro. "Dark shapes in the water, coming toward this barge."

"I don't see anything," said Flash, taking a look.

"They're beneath the surface," said Tun. "Unless I'm much mistaken, we're about to be visited by—"

"Mermen!" cried a voice up on deck.

Tun sprinted to the locked cabin door, hit against it with his shoulder. "I've encountered these devils before. A vicious lot I can assure you."

"They can breathe under water?"

"Aye," answered the lion man as he hit the door once again. "They live beneath the sea, and some tribes inhabit these wretched swamps. They ofttimes raid ships and barges, seeking both plunder and sport. They are amphibians and can live upon the land when they so wish."

The door opened suddenly outward, Tun went hopping into the small stairway.

Captain Norlag was huddled there. "We are beset with mermen." He held out Flash's pistol. "I cannot for the life of me fathom the working of this weapon. Can you show me? And hurry, sir, hurry!"

An agonized scream sounded on the foredeck. Thumping, splashing footsteps echoed.

Flash took the pistol and then noticed that the captain had his rucksack strapped to his back. Without warning, he grabbed the captain by the neck, pulling him down the stairs. "I'll take my belongings back."

Norlag stumbled and fell.

Flash ripped the rucksack free, then heaved the captain into the prison cabin. "Slide the bolt," he told Tun.

"Done. And now?"

Flash flipped him one of the spare blaster pistols. "I'll show you how to work this thing."

"We are to help these scoundrels repel the mermen?"

"We . . . " Flash spun.

A large, scaly shape was hurtling itself down the stairwell at him. The merman was pale green in color, his muscular body covered with fine glistening scales. His head was more reptilian than human, with a row of fluttering gills beneath each ear hole. His mouth was open in a snarl which revealed his sharp, narrow teeth. In his scaly right hand, he held a dagger.

Flash moved swiftly aside.

The charging merman, splashing the foul-smelling swamp water which still clung to his body, thudded down to where Flash had been an instant earlier.

"Drop the knife," Flash ordered, his gun trained on the merman.

"Nay, fool!" The merman sprang for him.

The gun crackled.

Before the merman hit the floor again, the upper part of his body had disintegrated.

"Aye," exclaimed Tun, looking from the remains to the pistol in his own hand. "This is a powerful weapon indeed."

Quickly Flash showed him how to use the gun. "If we leave the barge," he asked, "can you guide me to the capital?"

"That I can, though you still have well over two hundred miles to go, my friend."

"We'll take our leave now, then."

"As good a time as any," agreed the lion man. "I've never thought a river barge the best mode of travel."

Up on the deck were five more mermen fighting with the barge crew.

As Flash and Tun emerged from the stairwell, the nearest merman was about to slit the throat of a young member of the crew.

Shoving the blaster into his belt, the lion man leaped. He kicked the knife out of the scaly hand. He grabbed the startled green man, spun him once high above his head before flinging him over the port rail. "I'll save the gun for real emergencies." Tun was laughing a deep chesty laugh. "Ah, and here's another slimy lad looking for trouble."

Tun, in a great bounding step, reached another pair of combatants. Here, a merman had a stocky crewman pinned to the deck, a two-pronged knife raised above his head. "Back into the ooze with you, my boy," roared the lion man, his tail flicking like a whip.

He yanked the merman up by the throat. The merman, screaming in protest, went sailing high over the starboard rail. His flying body was finally lost in the thickening mist.

"Stay back," warned Flash.

A third scaly merman was stalking toward the laughing lion man. He dived at Tun's back, knife in hand. Flash thrust his blaster in his waistband. He leaped, caught hold of the man's shoulders. "You may as well join your friends," he said. He pulled the merman backwards, thrusting a knee into his spine.

The green man twisted, slashing at Flash with his knife.

Flash caught the knife hand, chopped the weapon out of it. He jerked the arm up behind the merman's back. Then he forced the man ahead to the rail and shoved him into the river.

Before the splash sounded, a scaly arm went tight around Flash's neck, pulling him back with choking force.

"Allow me to repay the favor," offered Tun.

The pressure on Flash's throat ceased.

He turned in time to see his scaly green attacker go spinning away into the night.

A moment later, there was a splash from the other side of the barge. "I do believe," laughed Tun, "that's the last of the mermen, going into the water on his own and saving us the trouble."

"Let's gather up a few supplies," said Flash, "and then follow his example."

Something howled, far off in the gathering dusk. A warm wind came sweeping down out of the hills, making dry leaves and twigs skitter across rocks and chalky ground. The trees were twisted, standing in tangled clusters at each side of the road. The hoofbeats of their horses sounded loud in the twilight.

"They will be safe enough where we sent them," Anmar was saying to Dr. Zarkov.

An hour ago, they had come to a crossroads and the sorcerers and the freed prisoners had parted company—the five men who'd escaped hanging to ride on to a place of temporary sanctuary, and the scientists and Zarkov to climb into the hill country to rendezvous with the hidden aircruiser.

Talking over his shoulder, Beltor said, "A highly successful escapade, Dr. Zarkov. I am starting to fear, however, that Ming's police may punish the other citizens of that town. They may pick five more citizens and execute them."

The burly scientist laughed, his laugh bouncing off the huge rocks and boulders they were climbing through. "I can guarantee you that won't happen," he said.

"It is the kind of vicious reprisal which would appeal to Ming," Anmar pointed out. "How can you be so certain he won't simply order new executions?"

"Because," said Zarkov, "he's going to think the public killings came off exactly as planned. I only wish we had time to try this gimmick on a few other towns."

"Gimmick?" repeated Brother Anmar. "A gimmick is . . . some sort of stratagem?"

"You bet it is." Zarkov hunched his broad shoulders, shifting a little in the saddle. "Before I beat it out of the jailhouse—after I decked the royal cop who came in through the front door to see what all the rumpus was about—I woke up the sergeant. He's in charge of the police in the town. Before I revived him, I made a small incision in his upper arm and then covered it over with a bandage out of my gear."

"What exactly," asked Anmar, "was the purpose of that?"

"It wasn't too tough to convince him I was a powerful renegade scientist," continued Zarkov. "After all, he could see what I'd done to his bastille. So I didn't have any trouble making him believe I'd implanted a little something under his skin."

"What?"

"I told him it was a tiny bomb, but powerful enough

to blow him sky high," roared Zarkov. "If he tries to remove it or even pokes it too hard, it'll go off. And I persuaded him I could also detonate it from a distance by remote control."

"Which you would do unless he turned in a false report about the executions?" asked Beltor.

"Right you are," answered the doctor. "It should keep him from knocking off anyone else for a few weeks at least. After that, he may start to wonder if he wasn't conned by Zarkov."

"It should work at that," said Brother Beltor.

The howling they'd heard earlier was repeated. It came from the growing darkness to their right, and a moment later from their left. They could see nothing in the darkening woods they were traveling through.

"What sort of animals are those?" asked Zarkov. "Sounds something like the *canis lupus*."

"There are legends about this part of the country," said Anmar. "I told you before that many on Mongo still believe in witchcraft and magic."

"What is it they believe about these hills?"

"They say there is a tribe of people dwelling here," said Anmar, "who can change themselves into wolves."

CHAPTER FOURTEEN

"Another night in this swamp and I'll have moss growing on me," said Tun with a prodigious yawn. He stretched his arms up over his head, swaying slightly on the huge tree branch where he'd slept.

Two branches over, in a fork of the tree, Flash was opening his rucksack. "How's biscuits and water sound for breakfast, Tun?"

The mist was thinning as the sun came up. The birds had been chittering for an hour or more and several new kinds of insects were up and about.

"I recall we borrowed a quantity of dried beef from the good captain's larders," said the lion man.

"That's going to be lunch."

"A lion man must start the day with more than schoolboy's fare." He reached out a knobby hand. "I'll take my share of the meat now, Flash." After he had devoted several minutes to his breakfast, Tun asked, "What is it you plan to do now, my friend?"

"I have to find out what's become of Dale," replied Flash. "So I have to reach the capital and reconnoiter."

"You will have a tough time of it," observed the lion man as his tail flicked at the hovering insects. "Though I know well by this time you can handle yourself, yet to go up against merciless Ming single-handed—it is a difficult path you have chosen."

"It's what I have to do," said Flash. "You're welcome to come along."

Tun shook his shaggy head. "Would that I could. But for a lion man to show himself in the capital would mean death, death sudden and sure. This tail of mine is most difficult to disguise." He scratched at his mane of yellow hair. "Since you have brought up the subject, Flash, I'll tell you I have been giving this some thought during the night. I think my best course lies in rejoining my people. There is little or no chance to raise the kind of support we need in these parts."

Swinging down out of the tree, Flash asked, "How far must you travel to rejoin them?"

"The country of the lion men lies a hundred miles to the south of us." After swallowing the last of his dried beef, the lion man jumped down to the soggy ground. "The best plan for my people is to unite with Prince Barin against Ming."

"Who is Prince Barin? I've heard him mentioned quite a lot." Flash adjusted his knapsack on his back.

Tun pointed. "A half day's march will bring us to a disreputable riverside town named Tintura," he said. "Though I promised to guide you all the way to the capital, Flash, I feel I had better part with you there and return to my own land." He started walking, tromping down the profuse giant ferns and scarlet flowers which grew in his path. "As to Prince Barin, he is the rightful ruler of this part of Mongo. Ming's coup forced his father from the throne and executed him. Barin was then still a baby. He is still only in his late twenties, I'd guess. He lives in exile in the Forest Kingdom of Arboria, where he has steadily been gathering followers. As more and more men find they cannot live under Ming's rule, they slip away to join Barin."

Flash swatted two bright blue flies off his forearm. "Would Barin be a better ruler than Ming?"

"Aye," said Tun. "He's an honest young fellow, believes in a fairly democratic form of government. The sad state the empire had fallen into was not his fault, but rather that of his late father and his advisers. From all I hear, Barin rules his forest domain justly and well."

"You sound as though you have some reservations."

"Not myself," said Tun, "but many of my fellow lion men. We are a fierce lot, as I have told you, and many of us tend to be stubborn and absolute in our thinking. We would prefer a true democracy rather than the democratic monarchy of a man like Prince Barin."

"Do you believe the best way of overthrowing Ming now is by joining forces with Barin and his followers?"

"Exactly, my friend." Tun slapped Flash on the back. "You have grasped a good deal about our political situation during your short stay on Mongo."

"Politics is politics throughout the universe."

"Aye, and even history teaches us that—" He shot a restraining hand out to halt his companion. Tun tilted his head back, sniffing at the still somewhat misty air. "An odd thing." He pointed to his right.

Flash looked in that direction. "Something over there?"

After one more sniff, the lion man said, "Aye, something I didn't expect out here in the middle of this wretched swamp. It seems to have had some sort of accident." Beckoning Flash to follow, he barged through a thicket of tall clattering bamboo.

Flash noticed the odor now. "There's been a fire," he said. "It's still smoldering."

Tun forged ahead through intricacies of vine and branch. "It was a vehicle of some sort, judging by the smell of the smoke. Perhaps even a flying machine. We'll go cautiously from here on, my friend, as it is quite near."

Slowly, they eased through the swamp, through the hanging shaggy vines, over the damp ground.

"There it is," whispered Tun.

Fifty yards ahead was a silver flying ship. It had crashed here in the swamp and the engine had caught fire. The nose end of the ruined ship was gutted, a blistered black. Jagged cracks filled the windows of the control cabin.

"No chance of patching it up for our own use," said Flash.

"Nay, though I had hoped perhaps." The lion man nodded at the wreck. "You see the insignia there on the door?"

There was a golden sunburst painted on the now dented side of the craft. "Royal Police?"

"That is Ming's symbol. This ship belonged to someone from the palace."

"We'd better check to make sure there's no one inside."

"They probably jumped before the crash," said the lion man. "But let us investigate."

They had traveled only another twenty yards when, far off in the swamp, a girl screamed.

CHAPTER FIFTEEN

Ming stroked one bony hand across the sunburst emblem on his cloak. Hunched forward in the ornately carved chair, he watched the glass wall of the room. It was one-way glass, allowing the emperor to see what was going on in the green cubicle beyond. "Very lovely," he muttered, "a very attractive young woman."

Standing beside Ming's chair was the burly Captain Hakes. "Aye, the moment I saw her, I said to myself—"

"Yes, yes," interrupted the gaunt emperor. His eyes narrowed further as he studied Dale Arden in the interrogation room.

The slim, dark-haired girl was alone at the moment. Hakes and his underlings had just left her after a long session of questioning. She sat slackly in the straight metal chair, her head drooped to one side, eyes closed. Her right arm dangled limply down and the left leg of her jumpsuit was torn, showing a long bloody scratch beneath.

"You were," said Ming, stroking his wispy beard, "perhaps a shade too zealous in your questioning of the girl."

"My zeal has never been criticized before, sir. It is my belief—"

Ming waved him impatiently to silence. "Still she seems to have withstood the ordeal rather well. She will make a splendid addition to Princess Aura's ladies-in-waiting." A quick barking laugh escaped his thin lips.

"Exactly what I told myself when first I espied her."

"Yes, I'm sure you did, Hakes." Ming pushed himself up from his chair. "I do not wish to do this lovely creature any permanent harm, yet I must know more about this planet she claims to come from, more about why she is on Mongo."

"They mean us no good, I am certain."

"No one means Ming any good," said the gaunt man. "It is one of the prices a man must pay for attaining the heights. I will venture to see if I can persuade her to talk a little more."

"Do you wish my help, sir?"

"No, Captain. We have passed beyond your type of inquiry." He moved across the observation room to a parlor. When he touched one spidery hand to the panel, it slid aside.

Dale lifted her head when she heard the panel shut after him.

"I fear you have been put through an unpleasant ordeal, my dear," said Ming as he approached. "Honor me by accepting my most humble apologies."

"Who," she paused to take a breath. "Who are you?"

"I am Ming," he answered with a thin smile. "Ruler of the New Empire and potential ruler of the entire planet."

"Then it's on your orders I was brought here and questioned."

"Nay, not at all. As soon as word reached me of what had been done, I hastened here and put a stop to it."

"I've been here several hours."

"Regrettably, the affairs of empire weigh heavily on my shoulders. It is one crisis after another and I only just now was free to be told of your plight, my dear." Ming seated himself in the room's other chair, steepled his fingers, and watched her. "I am here now, however, hoping you will accept my most sincere and cordial welcome to Mongo."

"When will I be released from here?"

"From this specific room? At once," he said. "Though I fear I must ask you to remain my guest in the palace for a time."

"As a prisoner."

"Nay, as a guest," replied Ming. "You must understand, my dear, your advent is a rare and wondrous thing. To have a visitor from a distant planet in our midst is most unusual. Earth, did you say it is called? Yes, to have a visitor from Earth is a marvelous thing for us all. There is much we can learn from you."

"I know. Your police have been trying to learn things from me for hours."

"Again, I must apologize. Some of my Royal Police can be overzealous at times," said Ming. "You are unaware of the unsettled conditions which exist in this part of the empire. There is much radicalism abroad, much fanatical opposition to my government. When harsh measures are resorted to by us, it is only because we have been provoked by the excesses of our opponents. This, of course, does not excuse the unfortunate experience you have undergone, my dear."

Dale sat up straighter. "I don't think I can quite accept your explanation," she said. "Your police told me many young girls were brought here to the palace, at your request. As to their ultimate fate, I imagine—"

"Yes, imagination is what it is," said the emperor. "You will find no more sedate a man in all the New Empire. I will have to punish any officer who has been telling ribald tales about palace life."

"I'll be more convinced when I am free to come and go as I please."

"Soon enough, my dear, soon enough." Ming smiled. "After all, you are a stranger here, entirely alone. Mongo will take some getting used to and I am perfectly willing to undertake the task of familiarizing you with my domain. Indeed, who is better qualified than I?"

"Very thoughtful of you."

"You are alone, aren't you?"

"By now one of your police must have told you we're a team of three."

"Only three?"

"As I told the captain over and over, only three."

Ming nodded slowly. "And your purpose in coming here?"

"To find out what Mongo is like," Dale answered. "We're financed by the PlanExplo Foundation to survey the remote planets which have not yet been touched by the official space programs of the major nations of Earth."

"Your planet is not yet ruled by one man, by an emperor or king?"

"No."

"Sad," said Ming. "Sad." He rubbed his fingertips across his sharp chin. "Who are the two who accompanied you, and where are they now?"

"Our ship was about to crash," Dale said. "Two of us jumped before that happened, the third stayed with the craft to try and save it."

"So you do not actually know the fate of your ship?"

"No."

"Let us hope it found its way to a safe landing. Even now my men are searching for it."

"Is there any word?"

"Alas, there is not." Ming leaned closer, watching the girl through half-closed eyes. "Who was the man who stayed with the ship?"

"His name is Flash Gordon."

"Flash Gordon, eh? I should like very much to meet him."

"I have a feeling you will," said Dale.

Morning brought rain to the hills. Dr. Zarkov was the first to rise. He'd been sleeping with his broad back against the trunk of a dry tree. The thin leafless branches couldn't keep the rain off him. He rose, shaking his head so the drops of rain which had collected on his beard would disperse. Massaging his spine with his rough hands, he went over to talk to Brother Igon.

Igon had taken the last shift of standing guard. "Nothing unusual to report," he said, yawning.

"They howled most of the night."

"Perhaps your reputation has already reached the hill country," said Igon, chuckling. "The wolf people may be afraid to attack."

Zarkov rubbed his hands together and looked round at the rocky hills. "I'd like to come back here sometimes and see if I can trap a couple of them. I've heard rumors and tales of shape-changers on a good many planets, but I've yet to come face to face with one." Remembering that he was again wearing a robe with a hood, he tugged the hood up so it protected his head from the rain.

"We'll reach our aircruiser in a few more hours," said Igon. "That rescue operation of yours, though certainly worthwhile, has put us somewhat behind schedule."

Rubbing his hands together again, Zarkov said, "I'm anxious to take a look at this weapon that's giving you trouble. I should be able to see where you lads went wrong."

Arms tucked up into opposite sleeves, Brother Anmar approached. "Good morrow, Zarkov. I trust you slept well."

"I always sleep well," he boomed. "Any place, any time, any position. After I clear up some of your more urgent problems I'll teach you how to control the portion of your brain which is in charge of sleep. Then you can turn it off and on."

"You slept soundly," asked Igon, "yet heard the howling?"

"Once you have your sleep gimmick under control," replied Zarkov, "you can snooze and listen to what's going on around you at the same time. And you won't foul up the dream mechanism with the Zarkov method."

"Would you care for a frugal breakfast before we continue our journey?" asked Anmar.

"That I would."

Less than two hours later, they were nearing a forest area. The trees resembled Earth pines and oaks, but were considerably taller. Dozens of golden gulls were circling above the high treetops.

"We're not too distant from one of the tributaries of the Great River," said Brother Anmar, "which is why there are so many seagulls in the sky."

The rain had ceased and the sun was showing again.

"You've got the aircruiser in this forest?" asked Zarkov.

"Aye, we are nearly to it."

They rode into the woods, using a wide weedy trail.

Finally, Anmar said, "We will see the clearing after this next turning. The ship is hidden in a barn behind the cottage. You'll meet several more sorcerers here, for they have been guarding the craft."

They rounded the turn and saw the clearing. The cottage was of unfinished shingles and thatch, the barn of whitewashed planking. There was no one to be seen.

"We're here!" called Anmar.

But no one answered.

CHAPTER SIXTEEN

Tun tore aside vines and brush with his huge hands. "We are getting closer," he announced. "Over this way, my friend."

"Easy now," said Flash as he followed in the lion man's wake. "This could be some kind of trap."

"Nay, I think not. Those cries for help sounded too real," said Tun. "I've heard a good many in my day and I can tell the real from the false. Aye, yonder is the girl!"

Clinging to a low branch of a gnarled tree by her hands and feet was an auburn-haired girl. Her tight-fitting two-piece flying suit was torn and muddied.

Watching the girl from below was a giant salamander, similar to the ones Flash had encountered on his way to the Heart & Arrow Inn. This one, however, was even larger and was a dull gray in color with patches of milky red. It, too, had fangs and a long flickering tongue. Its jaws were wide open, the forked tongue whipping toward the dangling girl.

"Help me!" cried the girl. "Is there anyone around? Does anyone hear me?"

"Your fears are over, missy," called out the lion man. To Flash, he added, "Let me see if I can handle this fellow with the help of this marvelous pistol of yours."

Before Flash could reply, Tun went stomping off toward the huge creature.

The salamander made a moist, fluttering noise as it

watched the girl, waiting for her to let go of the branch and fall within range.

"Hey, you ugly brute," shouted Tun when he was near the beast's right side.

The giant head lowered and inspected the approaching lion man.

"You'll cause no more trouble in these parts." Tun began to draw out the blaster.

The creature all at once thrashed out with its great long tail.

The tail slammed hard into the lion man's stomach, knocking the wind from him. Gasping, gagging, Tun went careening backwards. The pistol spun free of his hand as he landed hard on his back.

The salamander turned its attention to him, lowering its head.

A second later, its head was turning to soot. Flash had used his own blaster to dispatch the salamander.

"Thank," panted Tun, "you, my friend." He elbowed himself across the mossy ground.

The body of the giant salamander swayed, then tumbled over sideways. The jungle shook.

"Can't hold . . . " The girl lost her grip on the branch.

Sprinting, Flash caught her in his arms before she hit the ground. Setting her upright gently, he asked, "Were you alone in the ship?"

She brushed back her long hair, smiling faintly at him. "Yes, I was alone," she said. "You don't have to worry about rescuing anyone else. If I hadn't been stupid enough to lose my gun while I was jumping free of the flying ship . . . well, thank you. Is your friend badly hurt?"

"Not a bit, missy," said Tun as he trotted over to join them. "A lion man is hard to kill, though now and again you can knock the breath from him."

The girl glanced at Tun's flicking tail. "I didn't notice . . . well, let me thank both of you."

"You needn't be unsettled," Tun told her. "I am aware that lion men are unpopular in the palace. We can't always select our rescuers, though."

"Please don't be offended. I don't share the prejudices of those who rule Mongo. How did you know I was from the palace? Oh, yes! You saw my fallen ship." She looked up at Flash. "Do you think the ship can be repaired?"

He shook his head. "It's beyond salvation."

The auburn-haired girl bit her lip. "I wonder how I'm going to get back home."

"We're on our way to Tintura," said Flash. "We're traveling on foot, but we can see you that far."

"If you don't mind a lion man for an escort," added Tun.

The girl smiled at him. "I'd be very grateful if you'd both allow me to come along, and I'd feel much safer as well."

After a second, the lion man said, "My name is Tun and this is Flash Gordon."

The girl said, "I am Ilana. I'm a servant of Princess Aura."

"She lets you borrow her flying ship?" asked Flash.

Lowering her head, the girl said, "Well, not exactly. I get very restless sometimes, cooped up in that palace and, well, I take what I need to liven up things. Yesterday, I borrowed an airship."

"Will they make great trouble for you when you return without it, missy?" asked the lion man.

"Some, I expect," she answered. "I am, fortunately, a great favorite of the princess."

"I see," said Flash.

Zarkov discovered the blood.

"There was some kind of brawl," he said in his

resounding voice. "Somebody got knocked into the wall right here, then fell down into the straw."

The burly doctor, along with Anmar and Igon, was in the lopsided old barn.

The aircruiser was not there.

Igon was kneeling on the threshold. "The ship was rolled out," he said. "Yet there is no indication outside that they took to the air from the clearing. There are no scorch marks on the ground."

"Perhaps they rolled it down the trail a distance before taking off," suggested Anmar. He crossed the hollow shadowy barn to study the splashes of blood Zarkov had noticed on the wall and ground.

The big scientist jumped up and caught a roof beam. He pulled himself up to scowl at a patch of wall high up. "Somebody fired off a blaster pistol," he said as he poked at a soot-surrounded hole. "I'd guess they missed." He let go of the beam and dropped to the ground, scattering straw. "Any idea who pulled off this caper?"

Anmar said, "There are many possibilities."

The sunlight coming through the cracks in the walls made something suddenly sparkle in the straw near one of Zarkov's sandaled feet. "Ha," he said, scooping it up. "What have we here?"

It was a circle of gold.

"Earring." Zarkov held the thing up near his nose. "First time I've run across an earring with part of the ear still attached." There were bits of flesh and blood clinging to the gold ring. "Must have got yanked off during the fracas. Mean anything to you?"

Anmar took the proffered ring and glanced at Igon. "What would you surmise, brother?"

"The Scavengers," said the other sorcerer.

While examining the gold earring, Anmar said to Zarkov, "The Scavengers are a band of ruthless looters who hang out in a river town near here. They usually restrict themselves to robbing and stealing from the ships and barges that travel the river."

"They must have learned somehow," suggested Brother Igon, "that an aircruiser was stored here. Such a prize would be worth a considerable fortune in the underground markets."

"They wear trinkets like that, do they?" asked Zarkov.

"Aye, they are very fond of personal jewelry and body decoration," replied Anmar.

"Chances are pretty good then that the aircruiser was swiped by the Scavengers?"

"That is a safe assumption."

"You know where they hang out?"

"We have a pretty fair notion."

Zarkov nodded. "Well, then," he boomed, "let's go and get the damn ship back."

CHAPTER SEVENTEEN

Silver wasps buzzed above their heads in the muggy afternoon air. Sharp beaked crimson crows cawed at them from the branches of the giant trees.

With a tired sigh, the girl asked, "Could we rest again? Or are we fairly close to Tintura?"

Slowly, dropping back beside her, Tun said, "Still another five miles to cover, missy. We'll rest now if you've a mind to."

"I would appreciate it." She spotted a fallen log and went to sit on it.

Moving closer to Flash, the lion man said, "When I told you Tintura was a half day's journey, I did not reckon on our having a woman in our party."

His back to the resting girl, Flash said, "This may turn into a way for me to get to the capital."

Tun lowered his voice. "You have something in mind?"

"Will she be able to get in touch with the palace from Tintura?"

"Aye, there is a radio sending station there."

"When an airship comes to pick her up," said Flash, "I should be able to borrow it."

Chuckling softly, Tun said, "I'm quite sure you'll find a way, my friend. I may, in fact, linger in town long enough to lend a hand." His face clouded. "Be careful with this girl, though, for I sense she may not—"

"Well, I think I'm able to push on." The auburn-haired girl rose.

With a grunt, Tun moved on.

The girl took Flash's arm. "May I walk alongside you for a while? I'm really not used to this much walking," she said. "Court life spoils you after a while."

"How long have you lived in the palace?"

"Too long," she replied. "I often grow very weary of it all. When that happens, I wander off."

"Doesn't that annoy Princess Aura?"

"No. Well, not awfully much. There are a great many servants and only one princess. There are more than enough people to cater to her whims."

"You don't much care for her."

"She's all right. I don't think she really cares for all that pomp and foolishness any more than I do. If your father is emperor, well, you're obliged to live a certain way, aren't you?"

"What about Ming himself?"

"I don't want to talk about him."

They trekked on in silence for a time. A scatter of bright yellow moths swirled across their path.

"I've only just met you," the girl said finally. "Still I get the very strong impression you're"—she frowned, searching for words—"that you're unlike any of the other men I know."

Flash grinned, saying nothing.

"What territory do you come from?" she asked him.

"A distant one."

The girl's frown deepened. "And why do you travel with a lion man?"

"Tun has saved my life, I've saved his," replied Flash. "It's a good reason for becoming friends."

"Well, you've saved my life as well," she reminded him, "which means we are friends, too."

"It does, yes."

Her hold on his arm tightened slightly. "How do you come to be in the swamp?"

"We jumped off a river barge."
"What caused you to do that?"
Flash said, "We didn't want to be sold into slavery."
"Well, it was indeed fortunate for me you jumped ship where you did," she said. "Flash?"
"Yes?"
"When we reach Tintura will you allow me to take you and Tun to dinner? There are one or two relatively decent inns there along the river. We can dine together and then I'll make arrangements to get back home to the capital."
"I'd be happy to join you," said Flash.

The dining room of the Cold Harbor Inn was large, its stone walls painted a pale gray. Copper utensils and tankards hung from pegs in the ceiling beams. A fire blazed in the red brick fireplace.
Flash, the girl and the lion man were seated at a square table near one of the leaded windows. This was the first hour after sundown, and thick fog filled the narrow winding streets of Tintura.
Tearing a chunk of brown bread off the loaf in the bread basket, the lion man said, "A pleasant enough place by all appearances. Much pleasanter than that low bistro I was so unceremoniously heaved out of the other evening." He chomped at his bread for a moment.
The girl was watching the fireplace. "I really don't feel like going back to the palace quite yet."
"Don't you think you've been away about long enough?" Flash asked.
"Well, yes, I suppose I have." She smiled wistfully at him.
"Now in my home country," Tun said after an audible swallow, "we'd call this bread a trifle bland. For real bread, with some taste to it, you have to start with cornmeal. We grow our . . . Hey!" He stood

up so quickly his chair flipped over and smacked the wooden floor.

"Make no further moves, lion man!" warned the Royal Police sergeant who was striding across the room toward their table. He held a blaster pistol in his hand. Five other policemen accompanied him.

His eyes on the half dozen approaching police, Flash also got up from his chair.

"You should have stayed with your fallen ship, Princess Aura," the sergeant said to the girl.

She remained seated, lips pressed tight together.

"What means this?" demanded the lion man, his tail switching angrily back and forth. "So we have befriended the daughter of old merciless Ming himself, have we?"

The princess kept her eyes lowered. "I'm sorry."

"If you will but step outside, princess," said the sergeant in an overly polite voice as he touched his left hand to his gold helmet, "you'll find a flying machine waiting."

"I'm not sure I want to—"

"My orders, which come from our Commander-in-Chief, the emperor himself, are to make certain you return to the palace."

"I'd rather stay with my friends."

Toying with the clasp of his cloak, the sergeant said, "They'll be coming to the palace, too."

"Nay, not without a fight." Tun was easing one big hand down toward his borrowed pistol.

The sergeant fired his pistol.

The sizzling shot sliced the heavy dining table clean in half. One section toppled over onto the Princess Aura, tumbling dishes and utensils on her. The other half fell on Flash, sloshing him with soup and wine.

"My next shot will cut you in twain, lion man." The sergeant, with his free hand, helped the princess to her feet. "My abject apologies to you, princess, but I had to act to demonstrate my sincerity to these two so-called friends of yours."

"Why are you taking us to the capital?" asked Flash, using a white linen napkin to wipe himself off.

"Give all your attention to cleansing your soiled trousers," said the sergeant. "Men, escort these two handsome fellows to the airship. Try to keep them alive, but kill anyone who makes the slightest attempt to escape."

"What's the meaning of this?" asked Princess Aura.

"Had I my way, princess, I would shoot them both down here and now, especially that half human lion man," the sergeant told her. "I have, however, orders to gather recruits."

"Recruits for what?" asked Tun.

"The tournaments," answered the sergeant.

Most of the low wooden buildings of the little town extended over the river, supported by poles and pilings. The last traces of sunset tinted the low clouds a bloody red. A blind man in a tattered cloak was feeling his way along the muddy riverside roadway with a knobby cane. A large black dog came snarling out of one of the waterfront shacks and charged the blind man.

"Be off, mongrel," he said as he clouted it over the skull with his staff.

The dog yelped, retreating back into the dimly lit shack.

The blind man shuffled on.

"Typical small town," observed Zarkov. He lay hidden in a stand of huge oaks across the road from the row of buildings.

Huddled down beside him was Anmar. The rest of the men had remained with the horses a half mile distant. "The large warehouse there at the end of the row," said the sorcerer, "is the place wherein the Scavengers usually dwell. Lights burning inside. You can make out the glow through the shutters." He narrowed his eyes as he watched the big wooden building. It, too, was built out over the river and had a slanting roof of rough shingles.

The sunset glow suddenly left the clouds, the sky turned black and gray.

"Would they be likely to bring the thing right into their warehouse in broad daylight?" asked the doctor.

"This is a highly disreputable little town," replied Brother Anmar. "A goodly amount of loot, plunder, and stolen merchandise passes along that road and over the river." Anmar pressed his fingertips to his forehead. "I'll try now to read the mind of someone inside the warehouse."

Zarkov shifted his position, coming to rest on his side and one elbow. He smoothed his beard, watching alternately the Scavenger's hangout and the concentrating sorcerer.

"Ah, good," said Anmar after a moment, "I've contacted one of our own, Brother Orlan."

"So your boys were grabbed by this bunch."

Anmar didn't reply for a time. "You see," he said finally, "we can as yet only communicate telepathically over short distances. To get messages from far-off places, such as Ming's capital, for instance, the information must be relayed through several minds. Thus Brother Orlan was unable to let me know of their plight until I came within range."

"What does he have to say?"

"These Scavengers descended on our hideaway during the late hours of last night. The man on guard was napping, thus he was unable to detect their approach either physically or mentally." Anmar's hand remained pressed to his forehead. "All our men are alive, being held in the warehouse until the Scavengers arrange to sell them to slavers."

"They've got the aircraft, too?"

"Aye, indeed they have. They intend to sell it to a rebel group in the desert to the south. A fanatical faction, I might add, whom we have nothing to do with."

"How many Scavengers are inside there right now?"

"I'll find out."

Across the dark road, the black dog barked once more.

"Only three at the moment," said Anmar. "All together there are nine of them, but the rest have ventured to the other end of town to a slovenly inn. Our men are tied and in a loft above the main room of the warehouse."

"Loft, huh?" said Zarkov. "Any of the three looters guarding them?"

"No, all three are downstairs in the vicinity of the cruiser."

"Okay." Zarkov stood up, thrusting a hand into his robe. Under it was his flying belt. "Wait out here. I'll pick you up in the ship."

"What do you intend to do?"

"Go in through the roof," replied Zarkov, "free your boys, overpower the trio of crooks, and get your aircruiser back. It shouldn't take long."

"So think you?"

"I guarantee it."

As Anmar watched, the doctor left the ground, his hand on his flying belt. He drifted slowly up above the treetops. Then he flew across the street and landed on the slanting roof.

"What instrument is he using?" Anmar asked himself as he saw Zarkov kneel on the shingles and apply something small and glowing to them. A moment later, the doctor seemed to drop straight through the roof.

No sound reached Anmar from the warehouse.

On the dark river a flat barge floated by laden with bricks. A yellow lantern illuminated its prow.

Anmar moved a few feet forward.

The black dog, inside its shack, gave a low, mournful howl.

The side of the warehouse seemed suddenly to explode out into the night. Planks, shutters, glass went spinning, fragmenting, clacking together.

Out through the opening came the aircruiser.

"I do not have to guess who is piloting it," murmured Anmar, starting down toward the roadway to meet the craft. "Zarkov seems to have a particular fondness for knocking down walls."

CHAPTER EIGHTEEN

Down here there was no day or night. A damp darkness filled the twisting stone corridors and the low cells. On the floor of their cell was a scatter of moldy straw, and in an unseen corner, something continually dripped.

From around a dark turn in the dungeon corridor, an old man called out, "Fools, can't you see I don't belong here?" He repeated the question over and over.

"Aye, I feel much the same way myself," said Tun as he paced the gritty floor. His tail snapped aside wads of straw. "What think you, Flash—were we betrayed by that red-haired miss?"

"Makes little difference." Flash leaned his broad shoulders against their wooden cell door, arms folded.

"Aye, too true. Betrayed or not, we're caught good and proper."

Out in the corridor, a whip cracked. "Stay in line, you dumb brutes. Stay in line."

Torchlight blossomed outside. Flash turned to look through the small barred window in the door. "A parade," he said.

Two Royal Police came first, moving sideways with stun rifles aimed at the line of chained shuffling men. These men were huge, each well over seven feet tall, and stoop-shouldered. They wore only tatters of clothes and were covered with brown fur. Their faces were ape-like.

"Keep moving," said the sergeant at the rear of the line of the seven apemen.

A thin young policeman, his cloak two sizes too large, carried a smoking torch. Noticing that Flash and Tun were watching, he said, "No need to strain. You'll be seeing these fellows up close mighty soon."

The last apeman in line snarled, his sharp teeth glowing dead white in the torchlight. He swung one shaggy hand at the boy.

The young policeman stumbled back out of reach of the chained man, dropping his torch as he did.

"Stun the brute," ordered the sergeant.

Both of the stun rifles whirred.

The apeman froze, his teeth still bared.

"Pick up that torch, you young idiot. Next time don't go taunting the prisoners to the neglect of your duty."

"Yes, sir."

The sergeant took out a ring of keys and unlocked the stunned man from the string of apemen. He glanced over at Flash and Tun. "I'll have to leave your worthy opponent here and send someone to get him later," he told them. "Don't be frightened, he's going to be stiff as a log for many hours."

"It will take more than that poor lout to frighten Tun the lion man," said Tun.

"Aye?" The sergeant laughed. "You'll change your mind when you reach the arena."

"When are these tournaments to be held?" asked the lion man.

"Anxious for a fight, are you? Be patient. If all goes well, and I can get sufficient work out of these clumsy men of mine, this is your last day of life."

"Then the tournaments will be . . . ?"

"Tomorrow."

The glow from the spy screen etched deep shadows

beneath Ming's eyes, making his sharp nose more prominent. He was hunched in a highback chair, hands gripping the carved arms, studying the images on the screens mounted on the wall. "Anyone can be broken," he murmured. "This Flash Gordon may act calm and unafraid now. Once he is in the arena, however, the situation will alter. He'll beg and plead for his miserable life then." A chattering laugh came out of Ming, shaking his thin body.

The infrared cameras hidden in the cell brought the emperor clear sharp pictures of Flash and the lion man.

"Strut while you may, lion man," said Ming.

"Beg pardon, sir." A small round man in a white work smock came up and stood to the rear of the emperor's chair. He had a roll of paper under one arm, a sheaf of drawings in his hand.

Ming kept his eyes on the screen. "I can see why Dale Arden might be attracted to such a man," he said. "It's a surface appeal, nothing behind it and no intellect to speak of, I wager. Stop rattling those papers, Norber."

"Forgive me, sir." With his free hand, Norber straightened his rimless spectacles.

Ming's hand flicked out to shut off the spy screen. He rose up to his full height, turning to face the small round scientist. "What do you want, Norber?"

Ming's movement caused Norber to take an involuntary step back. "The gun, sir."

"What gun, Norber?"

"The weapon which was taken from the alien prisoner, Dale Arden. I've made tests, quite thorough preliminary tests," explained the nervous technician. "I haven't yet had time to get around to the other pistols." He held out his handful of notes and drawings.

"I employ, at no small expense, scientists such as

yourself, Norber, so that I may be spared the task of having to plow through a mass of technical trivia," said the emperor. "Just tell me what you've found out."

One of the drawings shook free of the pile and fluttered toward the glistening black floor. "Please excuse me, sir," apologized Norber as he bent to retrieve the drawing.

"Leave it be. Tell me about this gun, Norber."

Norber straightened. "It's considerably ahead of any hand weapon we now have even in a planning stage, sir. The microcircuitry is much more sophisticated than anything the imperial labs have come up with. And its range and destructive capabilities are quite fantastic. I made a rough chart to show the comparisons between—"

"Spare me the graphics, Norber," Ming interrupted. "Go back to your laboratory and get busy constructing a duplicate. I expect a working model by this time next month."

"Sir," said Norber, "that may be impossible."

"Impossible?"

"There's a memorandum here explaining, but, since you don't want to read anything, perhaps I could try to explain. It comes down to this, basically. There are three small components of this pistol which I cannot understand. What they are, what purpose they—"

"Get busy, find out."

"I intend to, sir. Which is why I've come to you." Norber pointed at the now dead spy screen. "If you could have that blond alien fellow brought to our labs so we—"

"No, he is to remain in the dungeon."

"He might be able to explain these puzzling parts to me. Otherwise, we may require long weeks of work."

"You cannot consult Flash Gordon."

"But—"

"Tomorrow you may interview Dale Arden."

"It's a rare woman who could understand—"

"She's a trained interplanetary explorer, Norber, with a good scientific background," said Ming. "Should she not be able to help you, you'll have to wait until we find the third member of their party, this Dr. Zarkov."

"All well and good, sir, but again it could involve weeks of waiting," said Norber. "It really would be much simpler if I could talk to Flash Gordon now."

"I have other things in mind for Flash Gordon."

"Oh, so?"

"He will die in the arena tomorrow," said Ming.

The aircruiser dropped gently down through the morning sky. Soon it was floating through a labyrinth of trees. Huge trees, with branches of incredible breadth, crossed and twined. And built in among the gigantic branches was a city.

"Even I," exclaimed Zarkov in his booming voice, "have never seen anything quite like this. Look at the size of those *chenopodium botrys*, and the *rheum rhaponticum*. Fantastic, fantastic." His beard rasped across the window of the passenger compartment as he studied first one aspect of Arboria and then another. "That's quite a trick. Quite a trick to build an entire damn city up in the trees, Anmar."

"It was begun several decades ago by a banished king," explained Anmar, "and completed by Prince Barin since his exile."

"Look at the size of those walnut trees," said the impressed Zarkov. "And what's that running up inside the trunk? Huh, an elevator."

"Arboria has several distinct levels," said the sorcerer. "Not graded by class, you understand, but by function. A quite complex system of elevators, ramps, and moving stairways links the levels."

Zarkov cocked his head far to the right, trying to see as high up as he could. "You've got guns placed up there above the city?"

"Aye, as a defense against an air attack by Ming. Thus far they have served us in good stead. The emperor tried two raids, and both of those failed. We have not been troubled from the air for many months."

Dr. Zarkov could see the citizens of the Forest Kingdom now as the ship cruised toward a landing area. They all wore clothes of forest colors. "Everybody looks young," he remarked.

"It may be the healthy life in Arboria," said Anmar, "though I suppose a goodly portion of those who have deserted Ming to join us are young in years. When one is older, there is oft too much to leave behind. And so they never make a move, no matter how cruel and repressive Emperor Ming grows."

"That's how they end up hanging from gallows in public squares," said Zarkov. "Well, sir, I've always felt free to roam the universe. You should never own more than portable property if you can help it. Though that notion is not original with Zarkov, it's still a good one."

A scarcely noticeable bounce told them the ship had landed.

The circular landing area was supported on an interlacing of huge branches and was pale gold in color. Standing beside the exit ramp was a middle-sized young man in a deep green cloak.

As Zarkov strode from the ship, the young man came out onto the pale gold landing area to greet him. "Dr. Zarkov," he said, "allow me to welcome you to Arboria. I hope your stay here will give you a better impression of Mongo and its people than what has befallen you thus far. My name is Marco."

After scanning the tree city which rose up all around him, Zarkov said, "Well, as long as I'm going to be a prisoner I might as well serve my time in pleasant surroundings."

Marco bowed his head for a moment. "Allow me to express the sincere regrets of Prince Barin for having had to recruit you in such a high-handed manner, Doctor. The problems we face, however, are such as to make it necessary at times."

"Just so you don't make a habit of it," said Zarkov. "Because if you get to believing that the ends justify the means, then you're not much better than Ming. I've lived somewhat longer than you have and in a good many more places. I guarantee you there's no such thing as a nice tyrant."

Marco continued to avoid looking Zarkov in the eye. He cleared his throat, saying, "Prince Barin is on a hunting trip at the edge of the kingdom and will not return for a few days. I have, however, been in communication with him. He sends you his good wishes, Dr. Zarkov."

The doctor asked him, "What exactly is your function in this setup, Marco?"

"I am," said the young man, "what you would call on your planet . . . Anmar, what is the equivalent term?"

"Public relations man," supplied Anmar.

"Ah, that explains it," rumbled Zarkov.

"Now," said Marco, his face a bit flushed, "Dr. Anmar will show you to your quarters, which adjoin the lab complex."

"I'd like too see the lab first," Zarkov told Anmar.

"Very well, come along." The rest of the sorcerers stayed behind with Marco. Anmar guided Zarkov toward an immense tree trunk at the edge of the landing disc. He reached out, pushed a button and the trunk slid open. "This will carry us part of the way."

Swiftly, the elevator shot up through the hollow tree. "Fantastic, fantastic," said Zarkov.

They left the elevator to walk across a connecting ramp to another immense tree. They entered that and dropped down two levels. Stepping from this elevator, they were in a long curving pastel green tunnel.

At the tunnel's end stood a door. When Zarkov and Anmar were three steps from it, the door was pulled open. A tinny voice said, "Hello, hello, hello."

Zarkov glanced at the opener of the door as he crossed into the large laboratory building. "Ha, a robot."

The metal man was five feet high, a dusky copper color. His head was a rough caricature of a human head. Bowing, he said, "Hello, hello, hello. I am at your service, service."

"I must admit," said Anmar, "that I have not as yet eliminated all the flaws in my mechanical man."

"Flaws, flaws," echoed the robot.

"Once I get your weapons in tiptop shape," promised Zarkov, "I'll overhaul your robot for you."

"Good, good, good," said the robot.

CHAPTER NINETEEN

Pennants and streamers were everywhere. Every tower, every spire of the vast capital city appeared to have a yellow pennant flying from it. Streamers of scarlet hung from street lights and window grills. Huge flags, each with a sunburst symbol, were draped from balcony railings. It was a bright, clear, warm morning. The streets were already crowded with people moving toward the tournament arena.

The huge outdoor stadium was circular in shape, made of smooth stone. Flagpoles, each sporting a sunburst flag, ringed its rim. The towers of the imperial palace showed beyond it.

Two Royal Policemen, young and thickset, marched down the main street against the current of the crowd. Their boots gleamed, their scarlet cloaks fanned out behind them. Pushing their way, they entered a large cafe.

The proprietor was in the doorway to the kitchen. There were thirty small white tables in the room, but only four customers. "Yes, gentlemen?" asked the gray-haired owner.

"Merely a routine visit, grandfather," said one of the policemen. "This is Tournament Day, you know."

"Aye, I well know. It accounts for there being so little business." said the old man. "And last week, I could get no meat or fresh—"

"On Tournament Day," said the other policeman, rubbing his stubby fingers over the gold armor of his breastplate, "the emperor wishes everyone to enjoy himself."

"I enjoy hard work. There is much work to do here."

One of the customers left his table, hurrying to the door. "I'll pay you tomorrow, Egon, he called. Now I must hurry to the tournaments." He left.

"A good idea," said the first policeman. "You others, go."

"You, old grandfather," said his partner. "You go as well."

"I have been to many tournaments in my life, under kings and princes and emperors," he told them.

The second Royal Police officer walked up to the old man and slapped him hard across the face. "You don't seem to understand, grandfather. The emperor wishes everyone to attend, so that all may see what happens to rebels and traitors to the New Empire."

The old man slowly untied his apron, letting it drop to the floor. "I will go," he said.

A murmuring grew in the wide street outside. Six chunky white workhorses were pulling a golden cage uphill toward the stadium.

"Look there!" exclaimed a plump woman in a patchwork cloak.

"I've never seen one before."

"No man will have a chance against one of those!"

Within the strong cage stalked two large tigers, roaring, yowling in protest at their captivity and their hunger, slashing at the golden bars. The animals were a rare breed, originally found only in the wilder reaches of the Forest Kingdom. Growing out of the forehead of each tiger was a single white horn, a foot and a half long and as sharp as a spear. Since Ming had come to power, these unihorn tigers were bred in the royal game preserve on the outskirts of the capital.

The cage rolled steadily uphill. The people climbed,

many of them reluctantly, toward the arched entranceways of the outdoor arena.

Ming's bony fingers tightened around Dale's bare arm. "What better way to learn about my people than by witnessing an event such as this, my dear."

"I'd rather stay right here." Dale was dressed now in a sleeveless floor-length gown of a style much favored by the women of the palace. "I'd like my own clothes back, too."

Ming raised his thin eyebrows. "I thought you had selected this lovely and most becoming frock yourself."

"Two burly women came in here and sat on me this morning," replied Dale. "They took my jumpsuit and left me this little creation. It was either wear this or nothing."

"Again, my dear, I must apologize for the overzealous nature of my servants," said the emperor. "You can not as yet fully appreciate how much it means to each and every one of them to serve me well. Now come along, my dear, it is nearly midday. We must go to the royal box."

"I don't want to go."

"You must, I really insist." Holding her arm, he guided her toward the gilded door of her chamber. "You will witness many unusual sights, I promise."

Resignedly, Dale allowed him to escort her down a series of lofty corridors, then through an underground passageway. In ten minutes they emerged into a large glass-enclosed box overlooking the arena.

Several members of Ming's inner staff, including Erik, were already seated there. A moment after Ming ushered Dale to the seat next to his, young Haldor brought Princess Aura into the box.

Ming drew his cloak tighter round himself before turning to speak to his daughter. "I am very pleased you've returned to the capital in time for this eventful day."

The auburn-haired Aura took a seat behind her father. "Your police persuaded me to come home," she said, "and Haldor persuaded me to come here."

Haldor smiled at the girl. "Like a spoiled child, Aura, you often pretend to dislike things you're really anxious to take part in."

"You're very perceptive, Haldor," said the princess. "I often wonder why you're not able to see your own assistants taking bribes."

"A gutter rumor," said Haldor, slouching down next to the girl. "If you persist in hanging around in gutters, Aura, you can't help hearing such things."

Ming rested an elbow on the rail of the royal box. Stroking his beard, he surveyed the crowded tiers of seats. "A goodly crowd," he said. "Every bench filled." He raised his right hand, waved it.

From all around the great oval arena trumpets blared. Uniformed men were stationed at ten-foot intervals, golden trumpets aimed at the clear blue midday sky.

Ming leaned close to Dale. "I have a highly efficient administration," he said. "Notice how everything is occurring on schedule."

"What," asked Haldor, "is the first event?"

"The traditional one," replied the emperor. "The procession of prisoners."

Trumpets sounded again, the fanfare echoing.

Down at the other end of the arena, a high iron gate swung open.

"You should have put someone in better shape to lead off," remarked Haldor.

The first prisoner onto the tanbark of the arena, a frail man in a tattered tunic, stumbled and fell to his knees. A palace guard goaded him with a spear.

There were fifty men in the line which came straggling out of the dark tunnel mouth into daylight. Some were battered and bent, shambling in their gait. Others strode forward, proud and straight. A dozen guards, armed with spears and stunrods, prodded the prisoners around the arena toward the emperor's box.

Dale suddenly sat up straight, inhaling sharply. She'd noticed the blond young man near the end of the line. "Flash," she said.

Behind her, Princess Aura echoed the name. "Flash."

Ming laughed.

CHAPTER TWENTY

Flash looked up at the emperor's box. The sunlight made its thick glass glare and sparkle. But he saw Dale Arden. He raised his right hand in a gesture of greeting.

"Here now, prisoner," warned a guard, "no waving at Emperor Ming. Mind your place and station in life."

Grinning at him, Flash lowered his hand.

Dale was standing up there, palms pressed against the restraining glass. She was saying something but Flash couldn't hear it.

Another girl appeared next to her.

"There's our princess," said Tun. "That slat of a man beside her is, as you've no doubt surmised, merciless Ming himself."

"Yes, I figured as much," said Flash. "He seems to be enjoying himself."

"Seeing others in pain never fails to amuse him."

"All right, you scum, back into the tunnel," shouted a guard. "You'll be back in this arena soon enough."

As they trooped back across the hot arena, Tun asked, "You knew the dark girl, too, my friend?"

"Yes, that's Dale, the girl I came to the capital to find."

"You kept your temper," said the lion man. "Myself, I would have gone charging up there."

"That wouldn't have saved her."

"I'm doubting we can do much to help her now anyway."

"I noticed two entrances to that box," said Flash. "And the arena wall is not too high to scale."

"You'd more than likely be dead before you reached the inside of the box," said Tun. "You saw the guards on either side."

"They can be diverted."

"Aye, I suppose they can."

A thin, harsh voice came booming out of loud speakers all around the arena. "Halt a moment, prisoners."

"Stop, you wretches. Hear you not the emperor?"

"What devilment now?" murmured Tun.

"Princess Aura, whom I know all my subjects love nearly as much as I do, has prevailed upon me to grant the prisoners one favor," continued the voice of the emperor. "Thus it is that I now make this solemn pledge to you prisoners. Any man who wins two events in today's contests will also win his freedom."

A few of the prisoners cheered on hearing this.

"Not bloody likely," said one.

"Only another way of torturing us."

"Why debate," laughed a guard, "not one of you is going to win."

"What do you think, Tun?" Flash asked his companion.

Tun scratched his yellow mane. "Ming cannot be trusted," he said. "Yet it is possible Aura has some influence on him."

Flash nodded thoughtfully.

"You can't do this, father," Aura insisted, her hand gripping the back of his chair.

He watched her out of the corners of his eyes. "It strikes me you're excessively interested n Flash Gordon, my dear," he said. "What will Dale Arden think?"

"You already know what I think," said Dale. "You're being absolutely vicious in—"

"Vicious?" The emperor frowned at Dale. "Did I not promise freedom to any man who was victorious?"

"Flash Gordon," said Dale, "Flash and all of us came to Mongo on a peaceful mission. You're treating him like an enemy of the state."

"I assure you I'm treating him quite well. In point of fact, these tournaments are among my gentler methods of dealing with dissenters."

"Flash," protested Aura, still standing behind her father's chair, "isn't a dissenter. He and Tun saved my life. I told you all this before, father, and still you—"

"Yes, you have told me all this before, Aura. I am quite weary of hearing it." He leaned forward, gave a signal with one spidery hand.

About half of the huge crowd of spectators applauded as a side gate of the arena swung open. Two apemen emerged, hunched, long hairy arms swinging. One of them lifted a shaggy hand to shield his eyes against the afternoon glare.

Next two prisoners were prodded out of their tunnel into the arena. The crowd grew silent, expectant. The only sound in the arena was that of the pennants snapping in the light wind.

An apeman snarled, growled, then went charging toward the two prisoners. They were both small men of middle age. A few feet from them, the apeman halted.

More slowly, the second apeman began stalking across the tanbark.

The prisoners remained on the same spot.

With a roar, the nearest apeman leaped, grabbed hold of one of the men.

The other prisoner backed away.

The apeman lifted the small man up high over his head, threw him full force against the stone wall of the arena. He jerked him up from the ground and threw him again.

Half of the audience cheered approval.

The man was a bent and broken heap on the ground.

Diving at him, the apeman tore at his throat with his teeth.

Dale looked away.

"You'll find the moment of the kill is the most fascinating part, my dear." Ming took hold of her face, sharp fingers digging into her jaw, and forced her to turn her head back toward the arena.

"There's one fellow who won't win his freedom today," remarked Haldor.

A moment later, the second apeman killed the second prisoner.

CHAPTER TWENTY-ONE

"They're saving us for last, I do believe," said Tun. He was seated on a rough wooden bench, his broad back against the stones of the tunnel wall. There were now only ten other prisoners left.

Flash stood near the barred gate, watching the arena. "No one has survived so far," he said. "It's so senseless."

"Aye, but you hear the people out there, hooting and hollering," said the lion man. Afternoon light touched at his feet and the swishing tip of his tail. "Sounds to me as though a goodly portion of them are enjoying themselves."

"You told me most of them are probably forced to attend. They may only be pretending to enjoy this, so as not to get in trouble."

"They could put an end to such sorry spectacles as this," said Tun, "if they but had the courage to shove Ming from his throne." He joined Flash at the gate. "Look you, there are thousands of people sitting there, allowing that tyrant to tell them what to do. Yet if they had the courage to turn against him, they—"

"Enough of such talk, lion man." A guard jabbed his spear point at Tun's side.

The lion man laughed, pushing the spear aside with his little finger. "What would you do to me, lout? Am I not already virtually sentenced to death in the arena?"

About to reply, the guard noticed his superior approaching. "Yes, sir?"

"Send the blond one and that son-of-a-she-cat in now," said the other guard.

"You've been standing too close to the contests," Tun said to him. "There's blood on your cloak."

The big bearded guard made a disgusted face, brushing at his cloak. "Where, where?"

The other guard unlocked the gate. "Out into the arena, the both of you," he ordered. "See if you can't give the customers a better performance than the last few cringing devils."

"We'll give you all a show, my lad," promised Tun. He squared his shoulders, went striding out into the sunlight.

Flash followed.

The gate shut and locked behind them.

The bodies of the last five men to die in the arena had not yet been removed. They were scattered across the tanbark, clusters of black flies hovering over them, large black buzzards circling, ready to peck at them.

"I know I'm a match for any dull-witted apeman who ever lived," said Tun. "And you can more than take care of yourself, my friend."

After glancing at the royal box, Flash turned his attention to the entryway used by the apemen. "I'm still wondering if Ming will keep his word."

"He stipulated *two* victories, mind you. So after we triumph over these fellows, we'll have yet another challenge to face."

"Here they are."

Two fresh apemen were in the arena now. The pair moved slowly, coming nearer and nearer to Flash and the lion man.

"By the seven blue eyes of the god of thunder," said Tun, "I hate this waiting around." He went running straight at the approaching apemen. "Look out, you numbskulls!"

Surprised, one of the apemen took a step back. The other kept coming, teeth showing in a twisted snarl.

"You look like the baboon with the most spunk," said the lion man. "I'll be taking you on first." He threw himself through the air, ducked the angry swing of his opponent's fist. He slammed a blow into the apeman's stomach, then a second and a third.

Flash, meantime, was approaching the other apeman. "I'll give you a choice," Flash said to him. "Go back into your tunnel, otherwise I'm afraid I'll have to kill you."

The hair across the apeman's back bristled. "Kill you," he howled. "Me kill you." He jumped for Flash.

But Flash was no longer there. As the apeman sailed by, Flash thrust out a booted foot, at the same time delivering a chopping blow to the beast man's thick neck.

The apeman fell on his face, gasping.

Flash circled him, caught hold of his arm and pulled him upright before sending him spinning away across the sun-bright arena.

To his right, he heard a bone snapping.

"Takes care of this fellow." Tun let the apeman, his neck now broken, fall dead. "Need any assistance on the other one?"

"No thanks," grinned Flash.

The surviving apeman, however, was not attempting to come near. He watched the body of his dead companion for a moment, scowled at Flash and Tun. Then he spun and ran from the arena.

The crowd, nearly all of them this time, roared.

The cheering continued for several long minutes. Finally it ceased, an anticipatory quiet filling the place. Every one of the thousands of spectators was watching the royal box.

Finally a voice was heard over the loudspeakers. "The emperor congratulates you," said Haldor. "He now reminds you that to win his freedom a man must survive not one but two challenges."

"Aye, we know that," said Tun. "Let's have number two and no more gab."

Another gate in the wall rattled open.

CHAPTER TWENTY-TWO

Two enormous yellow and black unihorn tigers appeared in the arena. They moved cautiously, bellies close to the ground.

The silence of the crowd held.

"Have you seen the likes of these rascals in your travels, my friend?" asked the lion man.

"Nothing exactly like them. The horns look deadly."

"Aye, that they are. With one slash of a horn, they can cut a man open." Tun watched the tigers, his tail switching in counterpoint to theirs. "Sharp as a blade they be as well. Still and all, we'll have no trouble withstanding the pair."

"Make that three," said Flash.

A third unihorn was emerging from the dark tunnel.

The crowd began to talk, low, frightened talk.

"Fellow in the lead's getting set to jump," Tun pointed out. "I'll take him." He galloped toward the first unihorn tiger.

The crouching animal's tail thrashed, its buttocks quivered. Then it sprang.

Tun dropped to his back on the tanbark. As the tiger shot over him, the lion man kicked out with both his feet.

The kick caught the beast square in the stomach, causing it to yowl and go slamming down to the ground on its side.

Tun was upon the animal. Locking one powerful arm around its neck, he grabbed for the sharp horn at its base. Gritting his teeth, Tun twisted. There was a crackling snap and the foot and a half long piece of bone was in his hand. "Now I have me a weapon," he said.

In a half-squatting position, he hopped a half circle round the partially stunned tiger and sank the horn in the animal's heart, killing it.

The second tiger ran by this struggle, green eyes watching Flash. It jumped for him without a warning twitch, clawing at his face and torso.

Flash swung, hitting a hard blow to the tiger's skull. He hit it again, even harder.

The animal went limp, toppling down on top of him.

Flash tried to roll away, but the heavy tiger had him pinned to the ground.

He heard growls and a roar. The third unihorn was beside them. It began to slap at Flash with one great sharp clawed paw.

Following Tun's example, Flash got hold of the horn of the stunned tiger who was holding him down. His strong wrist rotated back and forth.

The other tiger nipped at his arm.

Flash twisted harder. The horn snapped.

The other tiger continued to worry his arm. The beast's fangs pierced the skin of his forearm, drawing blood.

A satisfied purr began rumbling in the animal's chest.

Flash stabbed out with the bone horn in his hand. He lifted the improvised weapon and struck again. The second blow penetrated the biting tiger's skull and pierced its brain.

A few seconds later, the animal's large body collapsed, dead.

The dazed tiger was stirring toward wakefulness now.

Digging in with his elbows, Flash began to move himself out from under.

"Spare yourself the trouble." Tun was approaching the unihorn from the rear. He lunged, caught hold of its tail and gave it a fierce tug.

The tiger howled as it was yanked off Flash.

Keeping hold of the tail, Tun began to swing the animal. "Away with you now." He let go.

The tiger went smashing into the arena wall, its skull crushed by the impact.

Flash accepted Tun's proffered hand, got to his feet. "You got more than your quota," he said.

The other two tigers lay dead a few feet away.

"I am a very impatient man, as are most lion men," he said. "I'll tell you, I like this arena life a good deal better than I like being penned in a cell."

Hands on hips and head slightly back, Flash surveyed the arena. The gate to the animal tunnel had been shut. "If they aren't going to send out any more tigers, then I'd say we've won. Come on, let's see what the emperor will do now." He took hold of his companion's arm and they walked across the field toward the royal box.

The crowd, realizing no more tigers were to come, stood up and began to shout and wave their arms.

"They'll go free!"

"Free, as Ming promised."

A long stone platform stood immediately beneath Ming's glass box. Flash jumped up on this and grinned at the emperor. "I am Flash Gordon," he called out, "of the planet Earth . . ."

"And I am Tun, the lion man," said Tun jumping up beside Flash.

"We have won two victories and now claim our freedom," said Flash toward the box ten feet above.

Ming's breath fogged the glass as he leaned to look down at the two victors. Gradually, a smile twisted his lips, turning up the corners. "Here is what you have won for your friend and yourself, Flash Gordon."

The entire stone platform fell away like a great trapdoor.

Flash and the lion man went plunging down and down into the darkness.

The robot fell down again.

Dr. Zarkov glanced up from the diagrams and charts he had spread out on the work table in front of him. "One more of those clanking pratfalls," he warned, "and I'll overhaul you right now."

"Sorry, sorry," said the copper-colored mechanical man. "I was bringing you a snack, snack."

Rubbing at his eyes with one hand, tugging at his beard with the other, Zarkov scowled in the direction of the lab windows. The day had ended without his realizing it, night showed outside now. "I suppose I could do with a bite to eat. Bring it on over."

"Can't, can't," apologized the robot. "I unfortunately dropped it when I fell, fell, fell."

"Never mind then," bellowed Zarkov. "Go stand quietly in the farthest corner. I've just about got this weapon problem licked."

"Very well, well."

Zarkov had been working alone in the lab, at his request, since he'd arrived in the Forest Kingdom that morning. He bit down on the end of his pencil, bending once more over the scatter of papers in front of him.

After a few moments the robot said, "Hello, hello, good evening."

Zarkov looked up to see Anmar making his way through the tables and equipment toward him. "Don't say anything for a couple minutes," he told the sorcerer.

Anmar nodded and stood silently.

Three minutes later Zarkov pushed back from the table, rubbed at the back of his neck. "There she is, Anmar, all worked out on paper," he announced. "A few simple adaptations and you've got a whole new weapon."

Anmar studied the work Zarkov had done. "Why didn't I think of that?" he said finally.

"First thing tomorrow I'll tackle a real blaster cannon. Should be able to fix one up in next to no time."

"My admiration for your intellect is considerable at this moment."

"No reason why it shouldn't be."

Anmar touched his hand to the side of his head. "Forgive me, Zarkov," he said. "In my excitement at this impressive breakthrough of yours I've neglected to tell you the news I've brought for you."

"News?" The doctor's bushy eyebrows went up. "Something to do with Flash Gordon or Dale?"

"Aye," said Anmar, hesitating.

"Give me the worst. I won't pass out or burst into tears."

"Your friends are both alive, but they are captives of Ming the Merciless. This information has been relayed to us telepathically from a contact in the capital."

"Is that where Flash and Dale are now, in the capital of Ming's empire?"

"They were both there earlier today," replied Anmar. "It seems Ming held a tournament today in the public arena."

"Some kind of sports things, you mean?"

"Nay, it is sport only to a man such as Ming. In these tournaments Ming pits his political enemies against wild beasts."

Zarkov squeezed his right hand into a fist and

rubbed it against his side. "Is that where he put Flash and Dale, in the arena?"

"Flash Gordon only. Dale Arden was at the tournament, but in the royal box with Ming and his coterie. If she is an attractive girl—and I see from your mind she is—then it is highly unlikely Ming will execute her. He has other things in mind for girls such as she."

"I see," said Zarkov in a low level voice.

"Flash Gordon fought in the arena against apemen, and then against tigers," said Anmar. "He seems to have survived all challenges."

"That's Flash, sure enough."

"His exact whereabouts at present we don't know. Our informant believes he may have been returned to Ming's dungeons. At any rate, Zarkov, both he and the girl are alive."

Zarkov placed a hand on the other man's shoulder. "Anmar," he said, "I'll work on these cannons for you as I promised. After that I am going to work on a few new weapons for myself. Then I'm going to Ming's capital and I'm going to get Flash and Dale out of there. You and Prince Barin and every damn citizen of Arboria better not try to stop me."

"We will not," said Anmar.

CHAPTER TWENTY-THREE

Flash awoke. He was surrounded by a thick blackness. He remembered falling a considerable distance and landing on rocky ground. After that he had passed out. "Tun?" he called in a dry voice. "Tun, are you here?"

There was no response.

Flash listened, was certain he heard the sound of breathing nearby. He moved on hands and knees through the dark. "Tun?"

The lion man was stretched out on his back, breathing loudly through his open mouth.

Nudging him gently, Flash asked, "Are you hurt?"

"By the one beady orb of the god of the waters," exclaimed Tun faintly, "that was a fall, was it not?"

"A good twenty feet."

"From the feel of myself I broke nothing essential." Tun grunted as he sat up. "How did you fare, my friend?"

"A few lumps and bruises. Nothing more."

"Now you have seen for yourself how Ming the Merciless keeps his promises," said Tun. "And so have those thousands of cowards in the audience seen. Though it's unlikely they'll yet take action against him."

Flash said, "I imagine we're in one of his dungeons again."

"Aye, and we may have seen the last of daylight."

Flash had been squinting into the darkness in various directions. "Seems to be a very small glimmer of light over in that direction."

"Where? Oh, yes, I perceive it now."

"I'll go take a look."

"Be on the watch for further pitfalls."

"I don't see how we can drop any lower underground than we already are." Flash rose, felt out with his right hand. After a moment his fingertips brushed against stone. "Wall right here." Keeping his hand in contact with the cold stone wall, Flash worked his way across the room. "Yes, there's a door right here. Thick, wooden. It closes flush on every side except the bottom. That's where the light's coming in."

"Can you spy anything through the slit?"

Flash knelt, put his face down against the ground. "Stone floor out there, lighted by candlelight."

"Let me have a look." Tun crossed to Flash. He dropped down, placing his nose against the tiny crack beneath their cell's door. "Aye, we're in a dungeon. I get the scent of others locked away down here. Some of them have been here a good long time and one of them is several days dead."

"Which means we may not be getting much attention."

"Aye, perhaps Ming intends to leave us here until we starve to death," said Tun. "That would not be my favorite way to die. I . . . ow!"

"What's wrong?"

"I forgot I had put that tiger's horn in my belt. Just now I cut my wrist on it."

"Wait now," said Flash. "I think I had one in my hand when we dropped through the ground." Bent low, he felt his way along the ground. "Yes, here it is."

"So then we have two weapons," said Tun, "but no one to fight."

"We've got that door to fight," Flash said. "There's a good chance we can cut our way through."

Tun rubbed his hands over the rough surface of the thick door. "Indeed we can." He laughed. "Let us get to work here on this side by the hinges, for I feel no knob or keyhole on our side."

Flash joined him and they began to work.

An hour later the door rattled and was pushed suddenly open from the outside.

"Stand back," ordered the Royal Police officer on the threshold. Three other cloaked and helmeted men stood behind him. "Poor innocent babes, did you honestly think we didn't have your cell monitored with camera eyes? Turn over those weapons to me."

"You must fight to get them," challenged Tun, taking a backward step.

"Nay, that we will not do." The officer nodded at one of his men.

A stun rifle whirred.

The big lion man froze where he stood.

"You'll get the same if you don't follow orders," the Royal Policeman told Flash. "Now, give me that weapon."

Flash handed it over.

"Collect the one in your half-human friend's hand."

Taking the bone horn from Tun's stiff fingers, Flash gave it to the policeman.

"By the way," said the officer, "had you succeeded in getting your door open, you would have been killed the instant you stepped into the corridor. There are blaster beams trained on every door. Anyone who tries an unauthorized departure is gunned down at once." He gave a snickering laugh. "Please be careful in the future; we don't want you to die."

"Why?"

"Ming has much more in mind for you."

CHAPTER TWENTY-FOUR

Tun groaned once again. His left hand shook, his left arm began to swing down toward his side, his long tail snapped.

Flash had been long enough in the dark cell so that his eyes could make out the life-returning movements of the lion man.

The stun rifle had caused Tun to remain petrified for several hours. Flash had no accurate way of telling time, but he reckoned they had now been in their cell for at least ten hours.

"Tun, how are you?"

"Angry, mighty angry, my friend," said Tun in a croaking voice. "By the long red whiskers of the god of chance, to think I allowed those whelps to do that to me without even getting a hand on one of them."

Flash rubbed the big man's wrists and arms. "Still numb?"

"A trifle, but I'm getting control of myself again," said Tun. "For a bit there I could still hear and understand what was going on, then that ended. I was like some poor plow horse, sleeping on my feet." He stretched his arms over his head, causing his spine to crackle. "Did they bring us any food or drink during my catnap?"

"No, nothing."

"Then indeed Ming may mean for us to starve."

"The Royal Police gave me the impression Ming has something even more painful in mind."

The lion man stooped, rubbing at his legs. "You

know, my friend, I can understand why Ming hates me. It's only fair, after all, since the lion men hate him," he said. "You, however, are a pleasant lad come here to make a friendly visit."

"It must have something to do with Dale."

"Ah, I should have thought of that. Ming has no doubt taken a fancy to the girl. He believes he'll have a better chance with her if you are gone."

Flash's fists clenched. "I'm afraid that's it."

"Someone is coming," whispered Tun.

The footsteps were light, barely sounding on the stones of the corridor outside. They halted in front of the cell door. Keys rattled softly, two locks clicked, and a bolt was drawn.

The door swung outward. Princess Aura, wearing a full-length black cloak, with its hood hiding her auburn hair, stood there. She stepped into the cell. "Come with me quickly. I have an airship waiting," she said. "And I've seen to it the spy cameras watching this part of the dungeon won't work for the next few minutes. Come, hurry."

"Can we trust you?" asked Tun.

"Yes, yes. Only please hurry."

Flash took hold of her arm. "I can't leave the capital without Dale Arden."

"If you stay here you'll die, die by torture or under the claws of some dreadful beast. You must come with me now, Flash."

"You know where Dale is?"

Aura said, "Yes, she's in the north tower, in the women's quarters."

"Tell me how to get there," said Flash, "how to get there with as few people as possible noticing me."

"You'll never make it there and back alive. Come with me now."

Flash shook his head. "Tell me."

After a second's hesitation, the princess said, "Very

well. Here is what you must do." She gave him detailed instructions as quickly as she could on how to get from the dungeons to the north tower of the palace. "But," she concluded, "my father has special guards outside her apartment."

"Tun, you go with Aura to the airship."

"Nay, I would come with you."

"No," Flash said. "When I have Dale clear of the palace I'll join you. Aura, where is the ship hidden?"

"On the outskirts of town, near the river." She told him exactly where the craft was.

"Good luck to you then, my friend," said Tun. "We'll be waiting."

"Wait only an hour, no more." Flash stepped out into the corridor and moved away from them.

At the first turning, he went right as Aura had told him. Pacing off exactly ten feet, Flash reached up and pulled down on the iron candle holder mounted on the stone wall.

Silently, a section of the wall swung open. There was a stairway beyond, with an unlit candle sitting on the lowest step. Flash took it, lighted it from the wall candle and stepped through to the stairs.

The wall closed behind him.

It took Flash ten minutes to travel through the walls of the dungeon, across a concealed catwalk into the walls of Ming's palace. The air was hot and dry. He encountered no one.

Finally he reached the point inside the north tower that he was seeking. He located a stone flower on the wall and twisted it a full turn to the right. A narrow slice of wall swung inward.

Thick velvet draperies blocked his view. Flash listened for a moment before finding the slit in the drapes and parting them a fraction of an inch.

He saw the door of Dale's apartment and two guards seated before it, one on each side. The man on the left was slumped in sleep. The other guard had his cloak wrapped tight around him as though cold. He was awake.

Flash coughed. The guard didn't notice. Flash coughed again louder.

The man sat up, glancing around. He left his chair, and came cautiously down the marble floor of the hall.

Another loud cough brought the man directly in front of the drapes. "What is this I hear?" the guard asked himself.

Flash's fist shot swiftly through the parting in the drapes to connect with the guard's jaw.

Before the unconscious man could hit the floor, Flash had yanked him through the drapes and into the secret passage. Working rapidly, he bound and gagged the guard with strips torn from the man's own garments.

After borrowing his cloak and keys, Flash stepped out into the corridor, leaving the unconscious guard behind.

The other guard slept on.

Flash moved silently closer to the door. He got the correct key on the second try, unlocked Dale's door, and pushed it carefully open. He entered the apartment, closing the door behind him.

The dark-haired girl was at the open door to the balcony, watching the night sky. She turned, saying, "You're not supposed . . . Flash!" She came running across the thick white fur rug to him.

"It's taken longer than I planned to find you."

"Oh, Flash." She put her arms around him.

Flash kissed her, then gently pushed her back. "We've got to get out of here right now, Dale."

"They took all my things, so I will go as I am."

"Does Ming have Dr. Zarkov?"

"No," she said. "Didn't you rendezvous with him after the crash?"

"I was too late," replied Flash. "My guess is he was grabbed by someone, but if not by Ming's men, I don't know who."

Dale gave him one more quick hug. "Okay, I'm ready. We can talk later."

They had taken two steps toward the door when it opened.

Ming stepped into the apartment.

CHAPTER TWENTY-FIVE

The street was illuminated by floating globes of light. Each floated ten feet up, glowing pale orange, pale yellow, and pale green. Great leafy oaks lined the walkway, casting intricate shadow patterns on the paving and the mosaic stones of the wide street. A faint wind had risen and was blowing thin tatters of mist up from the night river.

Tun, wearing a dark cloak provided by Aura, walked at the girl's side. "By the three gilded horns of the goddess of fate," he muttered, "I wish we could move faster."

"We're out in the open now," reminded Princess Aura. "We don't want to attract attention by running."

"Aye, I suppose you're right."

This was a street of shops, small shops with bright awnings and cluttered windows. All the shops were dark, save for an occasional night light burning far back in the shadows. Fruit and vegetables were displayed in one window, swords and knives in another, a jumble of marine equipment in yet another.

"You haven't known Flash Gordon long, have you?" asked Aura.

"Nay, but I know him well. We have been through much together in a very short time."

"I suppose," said the girl, "he's in love with Dale Arden, very much in love."

Tun said, "He's traveled far and fought hard to find her. I would venture to say he does indeed love the girl."

"But he's never actually talked about it?" They reached the corner and she beckoned him to the right.

The river was in sight now. "Sometimes among men, especially among fighting men, Princess, such things are not spoken of. I don't exactly know why, though such is the case."

There was more light on the river side of this street. Several cafes and saloons were open and doing considerable business.

"The old wharf we want," said Aura, "lies about a half mile beyond this district."

"You could not have arranged all this yourself."

"No, I had some assistance."

Tun reached a big hand up under his concealing hood to scratch at his mane. "Then there may be some possibility of betrayal."

"No," the princess assured him. "There are people, a few yet, in the palace whom I can trust completely."

"Hey there, you two," called a blurred voice from behind them.

Tun slowed, stopped, and turned.

Two big men in the cloaks and helmets of the Royal Police were approaching them. The men had come out of one of the saloons and now crossed the street.

"What is it you wish?" asked Tun.

"Keep your temper," warned Aura in a whisper.

"You needn't tremble in your boots, my oafish friend," said the policeman who'd hailed them. "We are off duty, not on official business."

His companion laughed, swaying some as he did. "Aye, our only official business is to raise as many tankards of good green ale as we can."

"And that, oaf, is why we have detained you."

"Exactly," continued the other. "For we stand in need of a young lady to share the evening with us."

"You appear to be, oaf, in possession of a young

lady. Therefore, we must humbly request that you turn her over to us with all haste."

"Lest we shoot you dead in your tracks," the other added.

"A moment if you please," said Tun. "True it is that I travel with a young woman. I must warn you, however, she is my spinster sister and the reason for her long season of maindenhood is her extreme ugliness."

"She is ugly, say you?"

"Very much so," said Tun, "though it pains me to say such of my own flesh and blood."

"We shan't," said one of the Royal Police, "simply take your word for it."

"Nay, Sir Oaf, we needs must see for ourselves."

"I was about to suggest the very thing," said the lion man. "Step closer, gentlemen, look within the hood."

The two men moved, swaying, closer to Aura. Heads side by side, one reached out to push aside the dark hood.

Then the lion man acted. He reached out, banged their heads together. It produced a great crunch.

Before the policemen recovered from the shock, Tun administered chopping blows to the neck of each. They staggered, stumbled, and sprawled on the mosaic pavement.

"Now," announced Tun, "I believe we will run."

CHAPTER TWENTY-SIX

The emperor, tracing his moustache with his bony forefinger, said, "Flash Gordon, isn't it?" He allowed the door to close behind him.

"Yes, Ming."

"I should have suspected something, since the monitors in your cell haven't been functioning for the past half hour."

"I've come to take Dale away from here," Flash told him.

A dry chattering laugh shook Ming. "Have you indeed, my audacious alien visitor? You've come without weapons or allies in the foolish hope you might win out against me—against the Emperor. That is truly daring."

"So is this." Flash leaped at the saffron-robed Ming.

The emperor eluded him, drawing out a pistol from beneath his cloak. "You will die by your own weapon, Flash Gordon." The pistol crackled.

But Flash was flying through the air, low and under the blast of the pistol.

"You dare touch me," gasped Ming as Flash tackled him.

The two men fell to the floor. A marble table toppled over, throwing a heavy bronze lamp onto the thick rug.

Flash clutched the wrist of the hand holding the gun. "Let go."

"Nay, I will not," but Ming could hold on no longer. With a cry of pain, he dropped the pistol.

Dale ran over, grabbed it.

With a violent twist, Ming threw Flash off him.

Flash's head thunked hard against a corner of the fallen marble table.

Ming was back on his feet, pointing a spidery hand at Dale. "Return that to me at once, my dear."

"I'll use it on you, Ming, unless you stop where you are."

Flash, putting a hand to his head, tried to rise.

Ming continued stalking Dale. "I doubt, my dear, that a kind-hearted girl such as you will shoot a man down."

"I will."

Flash half rose, then fell back. His head had cleared, but he couldn't seem to control his legs.

"Will you?" Ming laughed his rattling laugh and reached out to take the gun from Dale's hand.

"Not just yet," said Flash, now recovered from his fall. He threw his shoulder into Ming, sent him staggering against the wall.

The emperor became tangled with the bright silk hangings which decorated the apartment.

Flash went after him, pulled him out of the draperies by his coat collar. He let go, threw a punch. It smashed against Ming's sharp chin, sending him into the wall again.

A pounding had started on the apartment door. "Emperor, Emperor," called the guard, awake now. "Is something amiss?"

Ming sat, dazed, on the floor.

Flash went to the balcony and took a look at the gardens far below. "Doesn't look like we'll be able to get out this way," he decided. "So it's back the way I came."

"Flash, watch out!"

Ming had regained his feet. He'd snatched up the bronze lamp and was charging at Flash with it.

Flash stepped aside quickly, but Ming couldn't stop in time. With a thin surprised yelp he went, still holding the heavy lamp, out the window and right over the balcony rail.

Running back into the room, Flash hurried to the door. Opening it a fraction, he said, in a fair imitation of the emperor's voice, "Come in here, fool. The alien is loose."

"I thought something must be—"

Flash knocked the guard out with one blow to the side of his neck. Before the man had completely collapsed, Flash had his cloak off. Draping it around his shoulders, he said to Dale, "We'll go now."

She took his hand and they stepped out into the corridor.

CHAPTER TWENTY-SEVEN

Tun paced the shed, then strode again out into the mist. He stood on the ramshackle pier, squinting at the night. "Still no sign of them," he said. "It is more than an hour since we parted." He went back inside.

An airship sat there, partially shrouded with canvas. Aura, hands folded, sat near it on a rickety wicker chair. "Are they coming?" she asked.

The lion man shook his shaggy head. "Nay, I see them not."

"We'll have to wait then."

"Aye, we cannot desert them."

Aura said, "I know you want to be free of the capital, too, Tun. Should neither Flash nor Dale appear in another hour, I'll fly you out of here."

Tun did not immediately reply. Finally, he said, "We'll talk of that later, when another hour has passed."

More minutes drifted by.

The lion man's tail flicked restlessly. He moved outside again. He heard footsteps on the planks of the old pier, but the fog still hid whomever it was. Tun's right hand rested on the pistol he had taken from the drunken Royal Policeman.

But it was Flash Gordon appearing out of the mist, grinning, with Dale Arden at his side. "Is all well?" he asked Tun.

"Aye." Tun laughed, coming forward to shake his friend's hand.

"This is Dale Arden," said Flash. "Dale, this is Tun."

"Tun the lion man, at your service," said Tun, with a deep bow toward the dark-haired girl.

"I saw you in the arena and Flash has told me something about you," said Dale. "So I feel we already know each other."

"Good." He led them into the shed. "What of your other friend, Flash?"

"Apparently Zarkov hasn't been captured by Ming's men," replied Flash. "I'll have to go back into the wilds and see if I can pick up his trail."

"Flash, you're all right." Aura rushed to him, caught hold of his shoulders and pulled him down so she could kiss his cheek. "I'm very glad."

Dale was about to say something but the lion man opened the door of the airship. "We had best be departing," he said. "Ming may learn we are missing at any minute."

As he helped Dale and Aura into the craft, Flash told Tun, "I don't think Ming will learn anything for a while."

"Why is that, my friend?"

Flash eased into the pilot seat, studying the control panel. "I'm going to need your help with this, Aura."

"I can fly the ship," she offered.

"No, I'll do it. You can, though, act as co-pilot."

"I'll sit in the back here someplace," said Dale.

After making the doors secure, Tun said, "You still have not told me what happened to Ming, Flash."

"I can tell you," said Dale. In a low voice she gave the lion man a brief account of what had happened in the palace.

Flash, with Aura's help, got the ship ready to take off. "Here goes," he said. The aircraft eased its sharp nose out of the shed, then lifted its long silver body into the air.

Tun scratched at his yellow beard. "By the multiple

ears of the god of rumors," he said, "I would like to believe that old Ming is no more and . . ." He suddenly remembered that Aura was Ming's daughter.

The princess turned in her seat. "What is it that's happened to my father?"

Flash said, "There was a fight, Aura, between Ming and myself in Dale's apartment. He fell from the balcony."

Aura looked out at the misty night for a moment. "He is dead?"

"I don't know. We didn't stay to find out."

"I see."

The airship was high above the city now. The fog hid the lights and the towers and the spires.

Aura said, "I really don't know how I feel."

"If I could have . . ." began Flash.

A loud bleating sound came from below their ship. An instant later, a similar shrill bleating started off to the left.

The princess reached out to grip Flash's arm. "Police ships," she said.

CHAPTER TWENTY-EIGHT

Voices called to them through the fog. Voices from above, from below, and to the side. The amplified words seemed to rattle the windows of their cabin.

"This is the Royal Police ordering you to land!"

"You have one minute to set down."

"We will shoot you from the sky if you don't obey!"

Flash asked Aura, "Our guns are in working order, aren't they?"

"Yes, but there's no need for them." She reached forward to flick a toggle switch on the control panel. She unhooked a mike and said into it, "This is Princess Aura. You will let me pass."

The answer came not out of the radio receiver, but again from one of the bullhorns mounted on the police ships. "You have forty-five seconds to land. Otherwise, you will be shot down."

"Didn't you hear what—?"

Flash turned off the radio switch. "They're not going to obey," he said. He ran his glance over the dials and gauges. "No way to get a fix on their position, huh?"

"A light ship like this isn't equipped for that."

"I think we've got three of them on us," said Flash. "And I think I can about guess their relative positions. So here goes."

He caused the airship to shoot ahead, accelerating rapidly as it gained altitude.

"I see the belly of one of them right above us," warned Tun.

Their craft passed close under the Royal Police ship, then climbed up in front of it. Flash banked, came down through the fog above the police ship. He pushed the gunfire button, the blaster guns on their ship's underside sizzled.

Tun pressed his shaggy head against a side cockpit window, laughing. "Got him. By the cropped tresses of the goddess of war, that's one out of the fray."

Flash had their ship climbing again. He began to execute a narrow loop. When he was at the height of the arc, he again activated the guns.

The lion man hopped to another window. "Another one down, Flash," he shouted. "Only one more left."

"I wonder," said Flash, "exactly where he is."

Something hit the body of their ship with a sharp thud.

"A torchman," said Aura, pointing. "They sent him down to cut open our cabin."

A man in a black tunic and leggings, wearing heavy suction boots and a flying belt, was walking along the scalloped left wing of their ship. In his gloved hand, he held a cutting torch.

"Nay, this will not do." Tun grabbed hold of the cabin door.

"Wait, Tun" said Flash. "Let me see if I can shake him off."

The man on the wing had turned the flaming end of his cutting torch against the wing itself.

"I'll shake him off." The lion man wrenched the door open, leaped out into the misty air.

He landed on the wing, legs spread apart, tail switching.

"He'll fall." Aura pressed her hands to her face.

The wingwalker swung his torch up to aim it at Tun.

The lion man surged forward, butting him in the stomach.

The suction of the boots broke, the man went pinwheeling away.

Tun looked up at the remaining Royal Police ship, thumbed his nose, and then dived for the cabin door.

Dale had anticipated his leap and was able to push the door open against the outside air pressure.

The lion man squeezed back into the cockpit. "Mind, don't let it slam shut on my tail."

Flash increased the speed of their ship again.

An instant later, the guns of the police craft crackled.

"Missed us," said Tun, "but they'll try again."

"We've got a faster ship," said Flash. "And, until they can call in reinforcements, there's only one of them."

In a shade over ten minutes, they had far outdistanced the Royal Police airship, leaving it behind in the fog.

Another fifteen passed. "We've lost them," observed the lion man.

"For now," said Aura. "They'll keep looking for me, whether my father's dead or alive. I'm now considered a traitor."

"You can go back," suggested Flash, "after we land safely someplace."

"No, I won't do that," said the auburn-haired girl. "I don't exactly know what I will do."

After setting a new course, Flash turned to the lion man. "We'll head for your territory first, Tun," he said. "After we set you down, Dale and I can start searching for Dr. Zarkov."

"He must still be alive," said Dale.

"Doc's nearly indestructible," Flash told her.

The ship continued on through the night.

After a time, Flash started to have trouble with the craft.

Tun said, "I fear we have a bit of a problem, my

friends." He had moved again to the window of the cabin. "That lout with the torch did something serious to our wing."

"You're right, Tun," Flash said. "We'd better land now."

"It would be wise to land before yon wing parts company with us."

There was no fog around them now. Only blackness everywhere, above and below.

Flash, with help from the instruments and from Aura, brought the ailing ship down through the night. "Not exactly sure where we are," he said.

The craft landed, bounced once, and skidded to a stop.

"Feels like rocky ground," remarked Tun.

"A very good landing, Flash," said Aura, pressing a hand against his arm.

Dale said, "What's our next step, Flash?"

He leaned back in the pilot seat, exhaling. "Might as well camp here in the ship till morning. It's probably the safest course."

"There's food and water back in that compartment there," said Aura.

"I'll fetch it," Tun said. "Then we'll have ourselves something of a victory celebration."

Flash said, "I hope a victory celebration is appropriate."

CHAPTER TWENTY-NINE

Tun awakened first. He rubbed his eyes, stretched, flicked his tufted tail. A frown creased his brow. "Can it be?" he muttered as he moved to the door and let himself out of the downed silver ship.

Feet on the ground, the lion man sniffed at the dawn air. He nodded, looking around at the dry orange and brown landscape. It was mostly rock, sandy ground, and gnarled leafless trees. "By the second head of the god of mobility," he exclaimed, "I do believe we're in lion man country!"

"What's that?" asked Flash, swinging down out of the ship.

"Good morning, my friend," greeted Tun. He stretched his arms out. "We did better than I'd thought."

"We reached your home territory?"

"Aye, we are here and I am home," said Tun with a chuckle. "I'll wager my village is not twenty miles from this spot."

"Then we'll set out for there," said Flash.

"It will be the best course to follow. For, once home, I am sure I can recruit several of my fellow lion men to help search for your friend Zarkov."

Leaning against their ship, Flash asked, "If Ming is dead, will things change on Mongo?"

"They may change," said Tun, "but not without a fight. You may be certain old Ming's underlings, men like Erik and Haldor, will try to hold on to power.

In fact, they may not even admit Ming is dead. Such things have happened in the past."

"You're still going to need a revolution," said Flash.

"Aye."

Quietly Aura climbed down out of the ship. She hugged herself, taking in the chill dawn countryside. "We're in lion man territory, aren't we, Tun?"

"That we are, Princess. I was just now telling Flash we are probably not more than twenty miles from my home."

"You needn't call me princess anymore," said the girl. "All that is over." She came a few tentative steps closer to the two men. "I guess I'm ready for a long walk. When do we start?"

"We'll have breakfast," said Flash, "and then get going."

"You're sure Dale won't need extra rest," asked Aura, "after the ordeal she's been through?"

"No more than you, Princess," said Dale as she joined them.

The afternoon sun glared hotly in the yellow sky.

Aura suddenly reached out toward Flash, saying softly, "I think I . . ." Then she crumpled, dropping to the dry sandy ground.

"Perhaps we should have waited until nightfall to travel," said Tun as he knelt beside the girl. "This is very rugged country to travel through." He uncapped his canteen and gave Aura a drink.

She sat up. "Got a little dizzy," she said.

With ease the lion man picked her up. "Allow me to carry you for a while," he said. "That way you won't mind the heat so."

"No, I . . ."

"Think nothing of it." He trotted on, with the girl in his arms.

"How are you doing?" Flash asked Dale.

"Despite what the princess may think about my stamina," said Dale, "I feel fine. Don't worry about my collapsing."

Flash grinned at her. "If you do, I bet Tun can manage both of you."

At dusk the heat began to fade. The sky began to turn a smoky blue.

Tun, no longer carrying Aura, who had recovered, sniffed the cooling air. "We are nearing my home," he announced. "But . . ."

"Something wrong?" asked Flash.

"Aye, there are strangers about," said the lion man. "Many of them, among my people."

"Ming's forces?"

After another sniff, Tun said, "Nay, I cannot yet tell. Come, we will approach nearer but with much caution."

By the time they reached the ridge surrounding the village of the lion men, the sky had darkened to a clear black. Now the noise of many people drifted up to them. There was much talk and movement.

"Await me here, my friends," said Tun. "I will venture nearer by myself." He left them near a scatter of dry trees and was soon lost in the night.

"Trouble?" Dale asked Flash.

"Hard to tell."

Tun came back out of the darkness. There was a puzzled look on his face.

"What's going on down there?" asked Flash.

"It seems to be a party," said Tun.

CHAPTER THIRTY

Several rough-hewn oaken tables had been set out in the streets of the village. Thick tallow candles in copper holders sat on the tables, flickering and splashing yellow light amid huge platters of meat, bread, vegetables, and loose piles of fruit and nuts. Further light came from a large charcoal fire over which an animal carcass roasted.

"By the wart on the nose of the god of joy," cried a shaggy red-haired lion man who was in the act of raising a mug of ale to his lips. "It is Tun come home."

"Aye, Nak," said Tun. "And I have brought friends with me." He gestured with an open hand at Flash, Dale, and Aura.

Nak clanked his mug down on a table top, hugged the returned Tun. "We have heard strange things concerning you, old friend."

Other lion men and women noticed Tun and began to cluster round him, hugging him, kissing him, whacking him heartily on the back.

At the edge of the group stood Flash and the two girls. The lion men's village consisted of curving rows of low mudbrick houses, with a few larger two-story brick buildings near the center. There were about two hundred lion men and women and children filling the streets of the village, circling the feast tables.

There were also some fifty men in tunics and tights of woodland green. Many of the men wore quivers of arrows on their backs.

"What exactly," asked Dale, "is everyone celebrating?"

"From what Tun said on the way down here," said Flash, "the lion men must have reached some kind of agreement with Prince Barin's people."

"Is Barin here?"

A tall young man with light hair and moustache turned toward them. "The prince remains in Arboria," he said. "I am Tomo." He held out his hand to Flash. "I'll hazard the guess that you're Flash Gordon."

Shaking his hand and grinning, Flash asked, "How is it you know my name?"

Tomo smiled. "You don't yet realize you've become something of a celebrity on Mongo," he said. "For though Ming has severely curtailed our use of the more advanced methods of communication, still there are many old and sure ways for news to travel. We have heard that you acquitted yourself well in the arena."

Flash said, "Yes, Tun and I managed to beat whatever they tried to match us with."

"He was magnificent," said Aura.

Tomo looked at her. "Is she your prisoner, Flash Gordon? I just now realized this is Princess Aura."

"No longer princess," the girl said.

"Aura helped us escape from Ming's dungeons," said Flash. "She is on our side."

"Perhaps this is an omen," said Tomo. "Now that the lion men have agreed to fight with us against Ming, I think the tide will turn."

"It's possible," said Flash, "that Ming is dead."

Tomo's eyes went wide. "What's this you say, man? Ming the Merciless dead?"

Quickly, taking him away from the others, Flash told Tomo of his fight with the emperor.

"I must communicate this news to Prince Barin," said Tomo, much excited.

"Remember," cautioned Flash, "Ming may not be dead. And even if he is, his high command may not admit it."

"Yes, I realize that." He was watching Aura a few yards away. "Are you certain the princess is to be trusted, Flash?"

"Yes, I am."

"Very well, I'll accept your judgment." Rubbing at his chin, Tomo said, "We have four aircruisers with us and tomorrow we will be returning to Arboria with the signed agreements which have been executed this day with the lion men. Will you come with us, Flash? Prince Barin will, I know, be most happy to meet you."

"I'd like to meet him," replied Flash. "Tell me, Tomo, since you have airships, do you also have technical facilities, labs and factories?"

"Ming has tried to keep all who oppose him in as non-industrial a state as possible," said Tomo. "Fortunately we have been able to set up a good number of plants and factories in the Forest Kingdom."

"That's good to hear."

"Is there some way we can aid you?"

"As you may have heard, we come from another planet," said Flash. "Our only chance of returning to our home is to reach our lab which is orbiting Mongo right now. Our survey ship crashed in the jungle."

"Yes, we were aware you had come to us from a far way off," said Tomo. "We should be able to help you repair your ship after bringing it back from the jungle."

Tun came bouncing up to Flash's side. He reached across him to shake Tomo's hand. "I am most happy that in my absence my people have had the sense to become your allies," he said. "I feel that all Mongo will soon be free."

"Yes," said Tomo. "Though it may require a long hard fight."

"Lion men like nothing better than a fight." Tun put an arm around Flash's shoulders. "Perhaps we can persuade Flash to fight along with us."

"We'll see," said Flash.

Tun looked approvingly at the feast tables. "The famine has so far spared us," he said. "So, by the six bleary orbs of the god of play, let us enjoy ourselves."

CHAPTER THIRTY-ONE

The aircruisers were large, forest-colored ships.

Tail switching and fists on hips, Tun was admiring the ship Flash would be traveling in. "Aye, it looks a sturdy craft."

"A match for anything the forces of Ming can put in the air," Tomo assured him.

It was midmorning. The plain on which the four Arborian aircruisers sat was hot and dry. A warm wind blew across it, rattling the naked limbs of the few dry trees. About fifty lion people had come out here from the nearby village to witness the departure.

Tun moved to Flash's side. "I feel I must remain here with my people for the nonce," he said. "There is much planning to be done, many details to be worked out. We shall meet again, though, of that you may be sure."

"I know we will," said Flash.

"Tell me, my friend, have you decided to remain on Mongo for a while?"

"I have to stay long enough to find Zarkov," said Flash. "After that, I don't know."

The other Arborians, in their woodland-green attire, were boarding the aircruisers. When the other three ships were loaded, Tomo said, "Come aboard, Flash, and we'll be taking off."

When Flash turned to give a hand to Dale, he noticed the princess was not there. "Where's Aura?"

"In one of the other ships," replied Dale.

"Why's that?"

"She's feeling gloomy this morning, wanted to be by herself for a while."

"Perhaps a visit to our kingdom will cheer her up," said Tomo. "She and Barin knew each other as children. Those were happier days, before Ming seized power."

Flash guided Dale up the boarding ramp into the big cruiser. He gave Tun a farewell grin and followed the girl inside.

The midday sky grew suddenly dark.

"Trouble ahead," shouted the pilot of their aircruiser.

An enormously loud flapping sound surrounded them. Tomo leaped from his chair in the passenger compartment and ran to a window. "A great flock of them, swooping down on us."

Flash and Dale hurried to join him.

"What are those things?" asked Dale.

"They're called harpibats," said Tomo as he watched the huge flying reptiles swarming outside. "One of the oldest surviving life forms on Mongo."

"Somewhat like the long extinct pterodactyls of our home planet," said Flash. "Only a good deal larger."

"They infest some of the remoter parts of the Forest Kingdom," said Tomo. "Now and again the notion strikes them to attack our ships."

The harpibats hooted and screeched as they circled the aircruiser, coming within inches of the wings.

Tomo had crossed to a communication panel and was giving out instructions. "Start firing at them," he ordered.

Through the open door of the front cabin, the pilot called, "Shall I take her down some?"

The blaster beams began to sizzle and crackle. A giant harpibat who had been diving toward their window was hit. His sharp green head turned to dust. Then another was blasted to soot as it swooped toward one of the wings.

"Prepare to land," Tomo told the pilot. "We're fairly close to Arboria."

"Flash, look!" said Dale, pointing.

A cluster of giant harpibats, their leathery wings flapping wildly, had circled another of the aircruisers. Two of the big flying reptiles dived straight into the piloting cabin of the ship. The cabin window exploded. The ship began to stagger, swinging in wild zigzags down through the sky.

"They've forced down one of our ships," said Flash to the preoccupied Tomo.

"I just called Arboria for some help," said the blond, moustached young man.

"Flash, I'm sure that's the aircruiser Aura is aboard," said Dale.

The injured ship was far below, out of control, heading for the treetops and interlocking branches which marked the edge of the Forest Kingdom.

Flash's ship was successfully holding off the shrieking harpibats. More and more of them were being destroyed. Their aircruiser had dropped a thousand feet.

"Clearing up ahead," the pilot informed Tomo.

"Yes, use it for a landing," he said. "We'll work our way back on foot and give them a hand."

"It's gone down," said Dale, watching the aircruiser in which Aura was traveling drop into the tangle of great trees. It crackled and smashed down through the foliage.

A few seconds later, it disappeared in the green cover of branches.

With one screwdriver held in his teeth and another in his right hand, Dr. Zarkov stood beside the aircruiser. He had been working on the blaster cannon in the ship's nose since a few minutes after dawn. There was a welter of tools spread out all around him on the hangar floor, very sophisticated tools and very simple ones. It was nearly midday now, and through the half-open door of the hangar, the trunks of the huge trees of Arboria shone a bright gold in the sunlight.

Zarkov made a 'huh' sound deep in his broad chest, then ducked beneath the airship nose. "There," he said, after making a final adjustment.

"Repast, repast, repast," announced a familiar tinny voice.

Coming through the door of the hangar was the copper robot. He held a tray aloft in one metallic hand. The tray was laden with dishes of food and a tankard of ale.

"Time for your midday repast," said the robot.

Zarkov dropped the screwdrivers to go running toward the mechanical man. "Ten to one he drops this, too," he muttered.

The robot's foot caught in a cable which wound across the floor. "Oops, oops, oops."

With a spurt of energy Zarkov reached him, grabbing the tray just before the robot hit the floor, face first, with a resounding clang.

"Ale, bread, some sort of cheese," recited Zarkov as he investigated the contents of the tray with his nose. "Meat—could be a hybrid beef—and these blue things must be tomatoes. What's this under the silver lid?"

"A helping hand would be appreciated," said the fallen mechanical man.

Setting his lunch tray aside, the doctor grabbed the robot by the armpits and pulled him to a standing position. "There you go."

"Thanks, thanks."

"Since I've finished my work," Zarkov told him, "I

think I will stop for lunch." He carried the tray over to the threshold of the hangar and sat down in the sunlight with the tray on his lap. He commenced eating. He'd just started in on his second blue tomato when an elevator door in a nearby tree opened and Brother Anmar came jogging toward him.

"Trouble?" asked Zarkov.

"What progress have you made?"

"All fixed," said Zarkov. "Haven't tested the damn thing yet, but I guarantee this blaster cannon will work several hundred times better than anything you boys have at the moment."

"Very good," said Anmar. "We've had word about your friends, Flash Gordon and Dale Arden."

Zarkov got out from under the tray and shot to his feet. "Where are they?"

"Heading for Arboria," said Anmar. "They escaped from Ming and were picked up by some of our people."

Zarkov eyed him. "But something's gone wrong?"

"The aircruisers in which they are all traveling are being attacked by a swarm of gigantic flying reptiles."

"That doesn't sound so good."

"We are sending a fleet of ships to aid them," said Anmar. "You believe this aircruiser is ready to do battle?"

"I guarantee it," boomed Zarkov in his loudest voice. "So let's get going."

CHAPTER THIRTY-TWO

Everything was upside down.

Aura was tumbled into a corner of the overturned ship. She rocked slowly from side to side as she tried to recover from the impact of the crash.

Up above her, the cabin seats hung down from the ceiling. The girl brushed aside her long hair. There seemed to be a faint haze around everything.

On hands and knees she moved across the floor, avoiding the light fixtures.

"Perhaps," she murmured, "if I get some fresh air I'll . . . feel better."

The glass of the compartment had popped out when the aircruiser had jammed down amongst the giant tree branches.

Aura pulled herself up by grasping the frame of the empty window.

Then she screamed.

A great scaly harpibat flapped at her.

The girl let go the frame, feeling dizzy. She fell—not back into the upside down cabin, but out.

She fell four feet, hit a thick branch, rolled off that, and careened down through thorny vines for another ten feet.

The sharp thorns slashed at her, tearing at her cloak, at the gown beneath.

She tried to stop her fall by catching hold of something. The thorns ripped at her palms and she had to let go and keep falling.

She fell further, slammed into a twisted lumpy branch, then over against the tree's rough trunk.

When Aura at last hit the ground and came to rest on a bed of immense dry leaves, she was again unconscious.

The harpibats still circled far above, screaming and crying, but they couldn't get down through the intricacy of branches and vines the girl had plummeted through. She was safe from them.

As she lay there on the brown and gold leaves with her cheek resting on her elbow, she looked like a sleeping child.

Then something stirred a few yards from her.

It was the large tendril of a huge spike-leaved plant. The tendril began snaking over the leaves toward the fallen Aura. Its underside was covered with purplish suction cups.

The tall, wide-shouldered young man in the forest green hunting suit drew an arrow from the quiver on his back. He was about to fit the shaft to his bow when a young man, cloak streaming out behind him, came running along the broad flat tree branch he was standing on.

"A message from Tomo," said the young man, panting.

Prince Barin lowered his bow. "Something urgent?"

"Aye, it is." The young man halted a few feet from the prince and his cloak settled around him. "Tomo just radioed to the palace. They relayed the message out here to our field radio."

"And what is the message, Harl?"

The boy took a deep breath before saying, "Their aircruisers were attacked at the crossover point between lion man territory and the Forest Kingdom. Attacked by a great horde of harpibats, one of the ships went down."

"Have defense ships been dispatched to aid them?"

"Aye, they are enroute at this very moment."

Barin nodded. "This will be a good opportunity to test that new blaster cannon the sorcerers have come up with."

"The ship carrying it is indeed among those speeding to Tomo's aid."

The prince said, "This hunting trip has brought us fairly close to the place where that aircruiser must have crashed, Harl."

The boy blinked. "Do you think it safe to attempt to reach them from here on foot?"

"Many places in the Forest Kingdom are not safe," said Barin, smiling. "Such considerations needn't hinder us." He signaled to the half-dozen men in his hunting party. "Come, men, we have a bit of work to undertake."

CHAPTER THIRTY-THREE

Aura saw it a moment before it reached her.

On waking, she first heard it. Slithering slowly across the dry leaves.

The girl raised her head and saw the enormous tendril of the flesh-eating plant coming for her.

She sat up, pushed her palms hard against the ground so she'd be able to stand.

The tendril kept coming, its purple-tinged suction pads making tiny puckering sounds.

When she got to her feet, she discovered she couldn't walk. Her right ankle had been sprained in the fall through the branches. If it had been only a question of the pain she could have made herself walk to get away from the carnivorous plant. But she had no control over her leg at all. She tried to take a step and fell to her knees.

The tip of the tendril touched her then, brushing at her leg.

Screaming, the girl struggled to pull herself out of its reach.

The tendril caught hold of her leg, pulling her back across the crisp dry cleaves. It wound itself round her leg and then her waist.

The girl cried out again, not with any hope of being saved, simply because she didn't know what else to do. Dressed as she was and traveling as a not-completely-trusted guest of the Arborians, she had carried no weapons.

She twisted as the tendril dragged her closer to the

huge center of the plant itself. She made fists of her hands, hitting at the thick tendril.

Aura didn't hear the footsteps at first.

The first indication she had of someone's being there was the smoke.

"Right into its maw," directed Prince Barin. "Thrust the torch in there. And hurry, light another one."

She saw the young Barin run by her with a blaster pistol in his hand. Beside him were two other green-clad men with torches. While the prince turned his pistol on the base of the grasping tendril, the men approached the body of the plant and stuck first one torch and then the other down into the large flower-like mouth.

A grating shriek issued from the plant. Then it began to shrivel, collapse on itself. The tendril went slack.

Barin came to Aura's side to help her up. "Your ankle's hurt?"

"Yes, I sprained it, I think." She held onto his arm, studying his face. "You're Prince Barin, aren't you?"

"I am. And you must be Princess Aura. We've come a long way since those days in the palace nursery."

"Yes, it was your palace then and my father and I were only occasional guests."

"And now," asked Barin, "are you and I enemies, Aura?"

"No," she answered. "I don't want to be Princess Aura any longer or sit on a throne."

He said, "You are welcome to be my guest again, Aura. We all live quite well in the Forest Kingdom despite . . ." He left the sentence unfinished.

"Despite my father," she concluded for him.

A clattering sounded up above. Barin looked up, pistol ready. "Ah, here comes someone to rescue you."

Climbing down from the crashed aircruiser above

were two of Aura's fellow passengers. Apparently, they had only now come to and realized she was gone.

Aura asked Barin, "How did you happen to be so near?"

He smiled at her. "Perhaps it was fate," he answered.

Tomo jabbed a finger skyward. "Look at that, Flash!" he exclaimed. "Have you ever seen the likes of that?"

Flash was frowning. "Matter of fact, I have."

Three heavily-armed rescue ships had arrived from Arboria. They were rapidly taking care of the flock of giant harpibats. One side in particular was eliminating more than its share of the flying reptiles.

Flash, an arm around Dale, stood next to their safely landed aircruiser and watched the conflict in the sky.

"What manner of weapon is mounted on that third ship?" asked the excited Tomo. "It disintegrates the creatures entirely, instantly. I've never witnessed anything like this before."

Another of the aircruisers, free of pursuing harpibats, was settling down to a landing in the clearing.

His eyes still skyward Tomo said, "Perhaps it is the work of the sorcerers."

"Who are the sorcerers?" asked Dale.

"As you know," answered Tomo, "Ming has tried to keep all his enemies at a very primitive level technologically. One of the things he did, quite long ago, was to make it a crime for any scientist to work for us. The penalty is death." The young man smiled. "Ming did not, however, make witchcraft and sorcery a crime. Mongo has a long and honorable tradition of magic."

"I see," said Dale, "so your scientists call themselves sorcerers."

"I'm certain it no longer fools Ming, but men of science like a joke," continued Tomo. "The scientists have enclaves in all parts of Mongo and they assist in recruiting men to our cause. They've come up with many new inventions, war-like and otherwise." He watched the sky once more. "It may be some new recruit who has devised this remarkable weapon."

"I wonder," said Flash.

The sky was clear. All the harpibats had either been destroyed or had retreated. The rescue ships dropped down to join the trio of aircruisers in the forest clearing.

Flash, taking Dale's hand, walked toward the ship which had been using the new type of blaster cannon.

Before they reached it, a side door burst open and a large bearded man in a green jumpsuit leaped out. "I knew it would outshine anything available on Mongo," he bellowed. "And it did. What'd you think of it, Flash?"

"A great breakthrough on the harpibat extermination front, Doc," said Flash, grinning.

Dale threw her arms around the burly scientist. "Zarkov! You're not dead."

"Dead?" he roared. "With my constitution and the diet regimen I follow?" He cocked his head at the ship he'd just left. "These sorcerer boys still have a thing or two to learn about synthesizing vitamins. And, would you believe it, they have never heard of Vitamin Z."

"The one you discovered and named after yourself?" asked Flash.

"That Vitamin Z, yes." Zarkov returned Dale's embrace with an enthusiastic bearhug, then shook both Flash's hands. "They've got a lot to learn. It was their good fortune that I convinced them to take me straight to the capital of Arboria. The only good lab setup in outlaw Mongo is there." He stood back a few feet, admiring both his friends, clutching at his beard. "I hear you've been giving Ming all sorts of trouble, Flash. Killing off apes, tigers, and lions."

"Only tigers," corrected Flash. "The lion men I made friends with."

"That old Flash Gordon adaptability," said Dr. Zarkov, in his booming voice. "Drop you anyplace in the universe and you always land on your feet."

"Speaking of which," said Flash, "they've promised to find our survey ship and bring it here to Arboria so it can be patched up."

Zarkov continued to tug at his beard. "Oh, yes . . . the survey ship," he said in what was, for him, a low voice.

"You don't sound very enthusiastic about getting it fixed," Dale told him. "Don't you want to get back to our orbiting lab?"

"Eventually," answered the doctor. "I tell you, there are several interesting problems I know I can lick right here in Arboria. The biggest of which is Ming. What can you do with a ninny who tries to outlaw science?"

"Ming may be dead," said Flash.

"Dead?"

Flash gave Dr. Zarkov the story of his adventures in the palace of the emperor.

When he was finished, Zarkov shook his head. "If the old boy is defunct, they're not letting on in the capital," he said. "We picked up a broadcast this morning purporting to be devoted to a fresh proclamation from Ming himself." He nodded at Flash and then the girl. He paused a moment, then asked, "Would you mind staying on here a while longer, you two? There's a good deal to be done."

Flash looked at Dale and she nodded. He turned back to Zarkov. "Not at all," he said.